The Divine Journey
from the ego to the sacred heart

Nikki Friedlander

AuthorHouse™
1663 Liberty Drive
Bloomington, IN 47403
www.authorhouse.com
Phone: 1-800-839-8640

© 2012 Nikki Friedlander. All rights reserved.

No part of this book may be reproduced, stored in a retrieval system, or transmitted by any means without the written permission of the author.

Published by AuthorHouse   8/24/2012

ISBN: 978-1-4772-1082-6 (sc)
ISBN: 978-1-4772-1081-9 (hc)
ISBN: 978-1-4772-1080-2 (e)

Library of Congress Control Number: 2012909378

Any people depicted in stock imagery provided by Thinkstock are models, and such images are being used for illustrative purposes only. Certain stock imagery © Thinkstock.

This book is printed on acid-free paper.

Because of the dynamic nature of the Internet, any web addresses or links contained in this book may have changed since publication and may no longer be valid. The views expressed in this work are solely those of the author and do not necessarily reflect the views of the publisher, and the publisher hereby disclaims any responsibility for them.

The man who follows the crowd usually gets no farther than the crowd. The man who walks alone is likely to find himself in places no one has ever been before. Creativity in living is not without its attendant difficulties or peculiarity leads to contempt; and the unfortunate thing about being ahead of your time is that when people finally realize you were right, they all say it was obvious all along.

You have to choose in life. You can dissolve into the mainstream, or you can be distinct. To be distinct, you must be different. To be different you must strive to be what no one else but you can be.

-Alan Ashley – Pitt

Contents

Acknowledgements ix
Prologue . . . . *xiii*
Chapter 1 1
Interlude, A Perfect Match *5*
Chapter 2 7
Chapter 3 11
Chapter 4 15
Chapter 5 19
Chapter 6 21
Interlude, Jewels of the Heart *25*
Chapter 7 27
Interlude, Early Rejection *29*
Chapter 8 31
Chapter 9 35
Interlude, Rumi Poem *39*
Chapter 10 41
Chapter 11 43
Chapter 12 47
Chapter 13 51
Interlude, Reality Sets in *55*
Chapter 14 57
Chapter 15 59
Chapter 16 63
Chapter 17 67
Chapter 18 69
Chapter 19 73
Interlude, Yoga Book *77*
Chapter 20 79
Chapter 21 81
Chapter 22 85
Interlude, Breakdown *87*
Interlude, Luca in Vietnam *89*
Chapter 23 91

Chapter 24 95
Interlude, Old Forge. 99
Interlude, Luca in Manila 101
Chapter 25 103
Chapter 26 107
Chapter 27 111
Chapter 28 113
Interlude, Waving Goodbye. 117
Chapter 29 119
Chapter 30 121
Interlude, Finding Meditation Space. 123
Chapter 31 125
Chapter 32 127
Interlude, Beginning Siddha Yoga. 129
Interlude, Luca in India. 131
Chapter 33 133
Chapter 34 135
Interlude, Going back to David 139
Chapter 35 141
Interlude, Leaving the Ashram 143
Chapter 36 147
Interlude, Luca Takes his Vows 151
Interlude, The Years Between 153
Chapter 37 155
Interlude, Goodbye to Dorothy and Max. 157
Chapter 38 159
Interlude, Renewing Wedding Vows. 161
The 10 Commandments for Marriage: 163
Chapter 39 165
Interlude, Adjusting 169
Chapter 40 171
Chapter 41 173
Chapter 42 175
Chapter 43 179
Interlude, Post-death Visit from David 181
Chapter 44 183
Interlude, Last Thoughts. 187
Epilogue 189
About the Author. 191

Acknowledgements

To those of you who have picked up this book, it all started with a book in 1967: *Yoga, Youth and Reincarnation* by Jess Stern. How many notes and 35 years of journals became this story is credited to Sarah Marshall Irvine, my content editor who toiled with an open heart for four years, as I write this, and traveled and transformed the life of this book. At the end, Patricia Wood, a sharp-eyed editor, pulled together this long-awaited experience.

This is a story about love and living in the heart, and how I experienced my own Divine Being. My guides and teachers were Margaret Coble, Dr. Ramamurti Mishra, Swami Muktananda, Gurumayi, Ram Butler, Drunvalo Melchizedek, Dawn Bothie, Bonnie Faith, Patricia Cota-Robles, Jennifer Berezan (Edge of Wonder Malta Tours), Robert J. Wade Maheny, Greg Braden, St. Germaine and Archangel Michael, and all of the heavenly beings that surround me.

All of these experiences came into my life with perfect and unexpected timing, and I just went for it. Most of these people are still with us, except Margaret Coble, Dr. Ramamurti Mishra of Blessed Memory, Robert J. Wade Maheny, and Swami Muktananda.

Proof readers and computer help: Bonni Tuscano, Carol Morrison, Dan Libby and Karen Kelly. Cover photo: Ellen Friedlander, cover design: Alexi Butts, Evie Hammerman, Karen Taylor, and Trudi Boltuch.

Sending Love, Nikki

The book is dedicated to:
Dorothy Reba Franklin Friedlander
The mother of all mothers

Prologue

Almost heaven real estate; that's what the locals like to call it! Pristine freshwater lakes, dense green forests, and the oldest mountains on earth, mountains where Rip Van Winkle can be imagined sleeping away the hot summer days. Sun pours in from the west, lengthening the shadows of the evergreens along the shore. This late July afternoon is in full radiant splendor—a spectacularly awe-inspiring event. It truly leaves one speechless as it seems to connect our heart to the oneness of all of life and the divine intelligence of the universe. Loons will be arriving shortly, making their eerie tremolo calls to add to the magic. Their plumage is what fascinates me: black collar, white necklace, so appropriate to offset their red eyes and the white checkering on their backs. Nature is quite the fashion designer, wouldn't you say? You will have to forgive me my digressions into fashion as I simply adore color, texture, fabric, and design.

 I gaze upon the lawn, yards of green velvet gently sloping to tan reeds. Trees embroider the lake, their branches reaching out in a warm embrace, a promise of shelter from the worst of storms. This is indeed the place where my soul feels most at home.

 The white dock is freshly painted, and a small red boat bobs gently in the wake of passing watercraft. Slowly down the channel glides a familiar antique Chris-Craft. I can't quite make it out through my clouded vision, but I know the bearded gentleman is squinting from under his weather-beaten cap in the lowering western sun. He guides the boat with one hand while his small fluffy white dog, Joe, sits perched like a sentinel on the bow. The two have traveled many miles over this route. As have I, as have I. My, how quickly time passes!

 The cataracts in my eyes make it hard to focus, and I see everything with golden haloes, a little inside joke between God and me! Literally and figuratively there has been a softening of the lens through which I see the world. I often experience everything as vibrating particles of pure energy, interwoven and supporting each other. What a 'magical mystery tour' we are all on! Mystery is what I AM, and we are the great creative force of life itself surfing on a sea of universal consciousness.

Writing this story is important to me, not in a psychological or mental way of making sense of my life, but as a reminder of our birthright on this planet as co-creators of the universe. For much of my life I felt cast adrift and buffeted on the seas of life, a prisoner of my cultural heritage. My childhood was difficult, as it may have been for many of you. This is not to complain; it's just the way it was. I had learning challenges at school and a mother who was, shall we say, not the easiest nor the warmest person one could meet. She did dress beautifully and made sure I was dressed beautifully, too. Maybe that's where my love of fashion and design came from. Our Orthodox household was fraught with rules that regulated daily life, and I was always afraid of doing something wrong. I married early—it was love at first sight—but I knew little about being a wife, and even less about being a mother. My wise and wonderful mother-in-law changed that for me. Staying married was a challenge, a tightrope I had to walk every day. Maybe I should have just joined the circus, I sometimes thought. At least, they had a net! But my dear, dear girls came from that union, for which I am eternally grateful. There were friends who helped me up when I stumbled, and amazing teachers who showed the way to wholeness.

It is only now that I can write this book. After all of my travels to inner and outer spaces, I walk free, grateful for the expanded awareness of the enormity of who we truly are. My hard-won freedom comes with a responsibility to contribute to others, and my story is that contribution. This is how I feel I can be of most benefit, by sharing what I have learned to be true—that we are all ultimately One.

Chapter 1

Esther's blond hair is cut in the pageboy she has always worn, and her jeans and classic white shirt set off her tall, slim figure. She is at home on these rolling acres, her haven since a red cardinal on a fencepost caught her gaze, causing her to slow down and see the lopsided 'For Sale' sign just below his perch. Surveying the land as she got out of the car on that distant summer day, her eyes lit up and her heart soared. She knew instantly that this would be her new home, the one she had always dreamed of, and indeed it had proven to be just that. Her love and devotion for the land was evident to everyone; the Bernese mountain dogs, the horses, her gardens, and her friends all thrived under her loving watch.

This particular afternoon Esther's attention was focused on Breeze, a two-year-old paint with thoroughbred bloodlines. The animal was very skittish and was proving to be quite a handful. With Jack, her farm manager, she maneuvered a rope around the horse's neck, but putting a blanket on her had failed again. Jack was convinced that Breeze had emotional issues, possibly from misuse. For a month he had stood quietly with her in the corral, coaxing her with special treats of molasses, flax seed, and oats. His efforts had born little reward. Today, after their latest failed attempt, Esther watched as Jack led Breeze back into her stall. She had an idea, though. Inside the farmhouse her husband, Arthur, and their close friend David were poring over architectural designs for a Jewish Community Center.

David wanted to build a state-of-the-art facility that would serve not only the Jewish community in town, but also be available to the population at large. Fifteen years before, David had been denied membership in a country club that was all Christian. His response at the time was to design a country club that accepted members without regard to race or religion. That same spirit of uniting the community still burned inside him. Apart from his business acumen, David was also known for having quite a knack with horses; and it was this talent that interested Esther today.

She had been so thrilled when her best friend Tori had married David. They seemed a perfect match: charismatic businessman meets New York fashion designer, both of them ambitious, community-minded, good looking. After they left New York for a quieter life in a small town, they raised two beautiful girls. Now, with Elizabeth and Kyle off to college, Tori had re-ignited her 'passion for fashion' that had been put on hold while the girls were young. The passion had ignited as a student when she was singled out in *What They Were Wearing*. The industry paper was covering a major horse show in the city; and Tori's original design, which she was wearing, made the front page. That fire had never been extinguished. But to her credit she had been determined that *her* girls would feel loved and nurtured. She had made them the focus of her life, obsessively so perhaps, and now equally as obsessively her focus was redirected to her career. It had taken only a few well-placed calls to people connected with the industry for Seventh Avenue to be clamoring for the promise of her new collection. *Vogue* had even offered a layout in their spring edition.

Esther leaned into the room where Arthur and David were working.

"I just can't figure this horse out, David. Have you two finished? Sorry, Arthur, you know it's just that David is so good with horses, and Breeze has been such a pain. Do you mind taking a look at her?"

Her eyes look beseechingly toward David, taking in his six-foot frame casually dressed today in Levis and ropers. Arthur and David exchange knowing smiles. There was no point in trying to reckon with this force! Arthur folded up the drawings as David rose to follow Esther.

"Now, tell me what you know about this horse," David asked of Esther as they moved outdoors. Esther shielded her eyes from the sun as she looked up at him.

"Well, Breeze is a two-year-old mare with some pretty good performance bloodlines, but she is very untrusting. Actually, Arthur has been after me to sell her because he is afraid that she will seriously hurt someone. She's already kicked Jack three times. But you know how I am—I always think that with love and the right connection, we can make her come around."

"What does Jack think about that? He's a pretty good judge of horseflesh, himself."

"He thinks she's basically a good horse but has emotional issues. He may be right."

"Not to worry! Let's go see what's distressing this little damsel. Maybe it's just the new digs she has not adjusted to, though I imagine her last home would be hard-pressed to match this."

David smiled and paused as he entered the barn. He loved that smell of hay and horse and leather, and he took a moment to enjoy it. As his eyes adjusted to the change in light, he moved slowly and purposefully toward Breeze, making sure to keep his gaze non-threatening. Everything about him exuded grace, confidence, and style. His voice began a low, soft drone of encouragement, "Take it easy girl. There you go, take it easy, girl. Nice and slow. There you go. You're doing fine." His charm coupled with his intelligence made him irresistible to animals of any kingdom, human and four-legged alike. In the barn or in the boardroom there were not many like him! It was truly like watching a beautifully choreographed ballet.

Breeze pawed the straw underfoot and made a token move to avoid the halter; but she, too, quickly fell under his spell. Masterfully he led her out of the stall and toward the mounting block outside to bridle and saddle her. After exchanging the halter for a bridle he deftly smoothed the blanket over her flanks and saddled her. It was amazing to watch the transformation. Hypnotized by the continuing lull of his voice, "Good girl. You'll be fine. There you go. There you go. Easy does it. There you go." Breeze allowed him to test his weight in the stirrup. Her ears perked, but she stayed still.

With one fluid move, he eased his leg over her back just as an explosive backfire from a passing pickup pierced the tranquil scene. The blast of noise set off an irreversible chain of events. A loud whinny pierced the reverberations of the echoing backfire. The Bernese dogs came to attention. Jack stopped his work. Everything had a dream-like quality. As if in slow motion the horse, now balanced on her hind legs, pawed through the air with her fetlocks. Fear and panic flashed in her eyes. David, suspended halfway up with nowhere to sit, released the reins and stretched his arms toward Breeze's neck. The bright blue sky with only a few puffs of cottony clouds were all David saw before Breeze lost her footing and fell directly on him.

Esther and Jack watched in horror. Time stopped, and it seemed an eternity before the horse scrambled to her feet and streaked out to the pasture, reins flapping. David lay on the ground motionless, eyes closed, breath coming in short gasps. Jack knelt and felt for a pulse, finding only faint intermittent movement under his calloused fingers. Not a religious man by nature, he let escape in a low tone, "Dear God!" Looking up into Esther's frozen face, he firmly directed her to go into the farmhouse to get Arthur and to call for help. She hesitated only a moment before she ran desperately as if to escape a nightmare. Everything was quiet now except for Jack's murmurs begging the Creator to spare their friend.

Interlude, A Perfect Match

A perfect match, that's what it looked like to the outside world. In fact, it was perfect because we both knew right away that we were meant for each other. Later on an astrologer confirmed this. She also made clear to me that the relationship would not be an easy one, even though the love was very deep. I knew on my wedding night that life with David would be very difficult. On the airplane to New York he was up and down the aisle with relatives; then the second day he lost his wedding ring, which seemed to make him happy. One night when I was feeling abandoned, I asked him how he felt about marriage. He told me, "Ninety - ten—you're ninety and I'm ten. You are the marriage."

Difficult? Yes! For someone like me who had such low esteem, it was just crushing. For a long time our routine never varied: David went to work and I stayed home. Whenever something went wrong, real or perceived, he erupted and I kept quiet. I fought back tears and bit my tongue to stifle words I wanted to say. It felt like walking on eggshells all the time. On one particularly difficult day, I said to myself, 'walking like this is for ballerinas, not the kind of dance we are doing here.'

But I must tell you, the man was charismatic. Everyone loved him, he loved the children and doted on them, and he bought me jewelry to make up for all the things he couldn't say. I first saw him in a restaurant in Old Forge when I was with my cousin. David was 'holding court' with a group of people he wanted to help him with a new project. Having been denied membership in the local country club because of his religion, he wanted to build one that would include anybody who wanted to join. Watching him win over the crowd with his personality, and then hearing his good ideas and enthusiasm, I could see that he was a born leader. He won me over, too; I just had to figure out how to live with this compelling man. That undertaking took a lot of time, work, and yes, sometimes heartache.

So, a match made in heaven—perhaps if you mean in the stars. Later I came to understand that the relationship was really about deep spiritual transformation that was bound to be gut-wrenching at times. The glue of love is the energy of the universe, and that is what held this marriage together.

Chapter 2

DURING the eternity waiting for the ambulance, Esther and Arthur had secured the area around David and administered to his needs as best they could. They were especially careful not to adjust his position on the ground. Mishandling the body after an impact injury could result in paralysis or worse; they both had been around horses long enough to know that. David had been barely able to speak with them, and it was clear that he was in shock. He felt no real pain and his concern was focused on Breeze. He apologized for what he thought would be the cause of another setback in her emotional healing. She had been progressing so admirably, and now she would be frightened and even less easy to handle. It was so like David to focus on Breeze rather himself. He gave Esther a reassuring smile and murmured, "It'll be okay, my friend, it'll be okay." She squeezed his hand gently and fought valiantly to radiate calm. "It'll be okay," she mirrored, "Yes. It'll be okay."

Jack stood out on the road ready to wave down the approaching ambulance. The barnyard was soon filled with an orchestrated cacophony of questions, lights, and people running, taking out equipment—the farm's usual peace taken over by trained specialists on a mission to save a life. Blurred images of EMT's kneeling on the ground checking David's airway, searching for obstructions and broken bones, bracing his back and neck all went by like old film footage in disconnected jumbled images. The crew radioed ahead to the hospital, and in a few minutes they were gone. Esther forced herself to concentrate on what needed to be done next.

"Jack, you'll go check on Breeze and call the vet? Give her some carrots and maybe some oats. Arthur, I can't believe this. I should have known something like this could happen. I should have. Oh God, I feel so awful."

"I know you do, Esther. So do I. Let's just get to the hospital as quickly as we can."

"I didn't even ask what hospital they were taking him to."

"Actually, you did, St. Elizabeth's. Thanks for taking care of things here, Jack. We'll let you know what happens."

"Arthur, what about Tori? We have to let her know what has happened."

"Let's wait till we get to the hospital. We'll know more then. Just make sure you have her number in New York with you."

Meanwhile in the ambulance the crew worked feverishly as they made the twenty-minute drive to St. Elizabeth's. They monitored David's vital signs as they inserted needles, administered medications, and performed CPR. David became increasingly pale and his breathing labored. Soon he was no longer able to speak and lost consciousness. The activity of the paramedics increased in direct proportion to the slowing down of David's vital signs. It was a profound shock for them all when his heart could not be restarted and his pupils were fixed. They had lost him. He was dead! A hush filled the emergency vehicle as the men sat quietly awaiting their arrival to the hospital. No matter how many times the crew lost someone, it was always a deep and very personal loss. Lifting David out of the vehicle onto a stretcher, one of them noticed a faint movement in his chest and an erratic beat began a tentative rhythm. Could it be possible? He had been without a heartbeat for over three minutes! Working with precision and speed, the emergency room staff took over while thanking the EMT's for their hard work and concern.

Run by the Sisters of Mercy, St. Elizabeth's was the oldest hospital in the area. Greatly in need of a facelift as it approached its 100th year, the hospital had served generations of townspeople and been witness to the countless vagaries of life. Its façade belied the care and healing that it offered inside. Most patients felt that the Sisters truly lived up to their name.

Arthur braked to a stop at the first empty space. He glanced at Esther for a minute, then drew a deep breath, pulling courage and hope out of the air for both of them. Together they ran for the emergency entrance. Just inside the door they were caught up short. It was that hospital smell. Pain and fear, anxiety and confusion have their own peculiar and pungent scent: an animal smell, like that of an unseen predator that can't help but alert and alarm the senses.

The clerk at the desk, busy with paperwork, hardly looked up as she asked in a not un-friendly tone how she might be of help. Words tumbled out of Esther and Arthur's mouths as they explained the accident. "He was just brought in. Can we see him?"

"Not right now. Please take a seat. Are you relatives?"

"We are not family, just good friends."

"Is he married?"

"Yes. His wife is in the city. New York. She's presenting a fashion show this weekend."

"I just need some basic information: age, address, any medical problems. If you could just put that on this form please, and let me know when you get hold of his wife."

Esther nodded and picked up the pen and started filling in the blanks as best she could. Surprisingly, her hand was steady, even though her mind was racing. Esther had been swept up in the storm of the accident and its immediate aftermath. She knew she needed to be calm and strong while they waited for the doctor's report, yet it was so difficult. People came and went in the busy waiting area: an earache, the flu, a broken hip, a head injury, a bicycle accident. Arthur and Esther grew increasingly uneasy as time passed with no update from the receptionist or the doctor. The chatter of people in the waiting room began to sound like background noise in someone else's movie. A clock ticked somewhere, measuring absurdly this void where there was no time.

"Should I call Tori now, or wait and see what the doctors have to say?" The words seemed to swarm in the air, not wanting to light anywhere like buzzing insects impossible to swat away. Her hand involuntarily went up as if to shoo them off. Of course she should call Victoria, and, of course, she should call the girls! A telephone, where was a telephone?

Before she could move, a stocky man in blue scrubs with a stethoscope around his neck stood in front of them. Neither Esther nor Arthur heard his rubber-soled shoes coming into the room. His appearance in front of their chairs brought them back to the immediate reality.

"Are you the ones who brought in Mr. Litchfield?"

"Yes." She could barely breathe. "What…how is he?"

"Are you Mrs. Litchfield?"

"No, they're our best friends."

"Have you been able to reach Mrs. Litchfield?"

"Not yet. She's in the city. New York. Can you tell us anything about David? I need to let her know, as well as their girls." Her voice was measured, but her hands betrayed her, clasping and unclasping to the beat of a galloping horse.

"He has to have surgery, but I will need her to sign for it."

"I am Mr. Litchfield's attorney, and also have his medical power of attorney," Arthur interjected. "The papers are in my office. Do you need them now?"

The doctor saw the anxiety on their faces. "Tomorrow will be fine.

Mr. Litchfield is on a ventilator right now and is being treated for shock. He is scheduled for surgery on a badly broken leg, and several ribs are broken. We won't know the full extent of his injuries until then. That was a large animal that fell on him and there might be some internal bleeding. We will proceed with the surgery. Will you two be staying here?"

"Yes. Of course! We'll stay until his family gets here. Thank you, doctor."

The figure in blue moved down the corridor. Esther always thought of blue as a healing color. Maybe this was a good sign. She hoped that was true.

"Come on, Esther. Let's find a phone to call Tori and the girls." Arthur gently assisted her to her feet. "Let's hope for the best," he said, giving her a hug.

Chapter 3

BACKSTAGE at the House of Victoria was the usual contained chaos that preceded each private showing: a babble of voices, the click of high heels, the swish of fabrics and the whirr of sewing machines making last minute alterations. Small arguments and pleas for lost items broke sharply through the steady flow of activity as stylists and make-up artists deftly transformed the faces of angular waifs into exotic beauties. Half-clad girls checked racks of outfits, mentally rehearsing their garment changes. Did they have their shoes lined up correctly? Did they have the right jewelry and accessories for each dress? In the midst of this commotion, a telephone's insistent ring sounded. Tori's assistant, Mindy, her hands full of papers, tried to ignore it, but the ring continued and she picked up.

"TORI, you have a phone call. It's urgent!"

"*This* is urgent, can't you see that? We start in ten minutes! Don't be ridiculous. I don't have time to take a phone call right now, not even if it were the president of the United States!"

Mindy watched with admiration for Tori as she moved fluidly from one model to another, checking the hem of one skirt, the bodice on another. Tori's deft fingers made the adjustments as she looked critically at each of the models and their outfits. Taking a hat off one and putting it on another, correcting someone's posture, Tori was fiercely intense. She looked everywhere at once and saw everything, yet saw no one.

"Tell whoever it is I will get back to them later!"

With long chestnut hair that had auburn highlights in the summer, and sparkling green eyes accented with dark eyelashes, Mindy could almost have been a model herself. She lacked only a couple of inches in height. Mindy's loss had been Tori's gain as Mindy was an exceptional assistant. She was always on the ball and three steps ahead of Tori, which was saying a lot.

"Tori is so busy right now. I am sorry she can't come to the phone. The show goes on in ten minutes. I am sure you understand. Do you want to leave a message?" Mindy's eyes widened as she listened to the reply. "Oh dear, Esther! I'll be sure to have Tori call you back as soon as possible.

Thank you for calling. I am so glad you are there. I promise I will have Tori call the second she is free." Slowly she placed the phone in its cradle gathering her thoughts. She would not tell Tori right now what Esther had told her. That would be disastrous. But was that the right decision? Was it her decision to *not* inform her boss that her husband was in the hospital? At the moment, however, she chose to push that thought as far from her mind as she could. She needed to make sure the show went on without a hitch and that her boss remained focused. She forced a faint smile on her face as she turned back toward Tori.

"Where is that teal green dress and the plaid brocade jacket? You are wearing that one first, Natayla! Those shoes you have on go with the black chiffon! Someone help her, please! We need more eyeliner on Carol. We want the make-up on the edge of exotic. I love the pale pink lips, though. Bravo. Gorgeous, darling! I need Anna Mae *now*. That strap needs to be fixed before Natalya goes out on the runway. Where is she? Luca, are the lights adjusted properly? I want to be able to see the shoes and the dresses this time."

Tori's talents were unquestionable. She had vision, determination and ambition—all necessary traits for success as a fashion designer. It didn't hurt that she herself was an exotic beauty with silky black hair, deep brown eyes, and a model's physique. She also had that bit of 'craziness' that made superstars in a profession that demanded one's personality match the uniqueness of one's vision. Popular opinion was something that Tori loved to influence. That it changed at a moment's notice and demanded constant vigilance was stressful but a challenge that she relished.

"Where are you, Mindy?" Tori called. She looked around. "Are the girls all lined up? Did the lights get adjusted, Luca? All right, beauties! Is everybody ready? Do you have all your accessories? Molly, that scarf goes on your head not around your shoulders; and larger, I want larger earrings with that outfit. Mr. Fairchild is out front, and they are ready with the cameras for videotaping. It is going to be fabulous! He *is* out front isn't he? He had better be. He promised me he was coming."

"Everything is in place, Tori."

"What took you so long? Were you on the phone all that time?"

Then Tori, distracted by an evening jacket that wasn't hanging right, rushed over to adjust it as the first model was about to enter the runway.

Three tall black scrims created a temporary 'theater' within the design studio, and a long runway covered in white with two rows of folding chairs on either side had been set up for the invited guests. Photographers stood waiting with four and five cameras around their necks, while tuxedoed waiters passed out glasses of champagne. Tori herself was dressed in a bold cheetah ensemble complete with shoes, tights, dress, hat and jacket. The fashion world demanded eccentricity, and she was always willing to accommodate and do whatever it took to promote her designs.

Chapter 4

Elizabeth and Kyle ran toward the hospital emergency room and yanked open the door. Unsure which way to go, they approached the reception desk as Esther spied them. The girls were tall, with striking good looks, and were dressed in stylish shorts and shirts befitting conservative young women in college. Tori was proud of her daughters and their wardrobe choices, horrified by the fringe and bellbottoms that were all the rage among the youth in America.

"Over here, girls," Esther called as she and Arthur rose to give them each a hug. "I'm glad your school was able to get hold of you so fast." The sight of Esther's familiar face brought a moment of calm to both of them, just as it had so many times over the years. No matter what the emergency, it was always Esther's sure hand that helped allay fears and smooth troubled waters. Her countenance and strength did this again, though this time her quivering smile betrayed her as she guided the girls to a more secluded corner.

"Esther, Esther, what's wrong with Dad? Is he all right? What happened? Where is he? Is he okay?"

"Let's sit down, girls, and I'll tell you what I know."

"So we *can't* see him?"

"That's right. The doctor will come and tell us when he's out of surgery and ready for visitors. Let's all go get something to eat in the meantime." There was something comforting about the normalcy of all of them eating together, as their families had done so often over the years, but that was where the normalcy ended. Evening in the emergency room has a peculiar quality as the lighting takes on a harsher luminescence in contrast to the growing darkness outside. The fluorescent lights, sterile décor, and cold tile floors had a hypnotizing effect as the little group stood vigil for David. There had been an unspoken agreement that no one was going home; and as the hours dragged on with no word, it was difficult to sleep. Gratefully, just before midnight the surgeon had come to say the surgery had been a success and the patient was in ICU, better left to rest without visitors until the morning. After that it seemed like only minutes passed before they were awakened by the morning hospital shift change. Arthur was the first to stand and stretch.

"I'll go get coffee for us," he offered.

"I'll go with you," Kyle volunteered.

This morning the coffee was hot and strong, and they drank it in silence. "When do you think we can go see Dad?" Elizabeth asked. "It's just so…" and she began to cry. Esther put her arms around her, feeling like crying, too, but determined to stay strong for the girls. "Your dad will be fine. Let's try not to worry and just send him lots of love. That helps people heal, you know." Just then the doctor appeared, last night's blue scrubs switched for a pair of slacks and nice shirt; he was on his way to the office after rounds.

"Your dad is doing better this morning. In fact, he's been moved to a private room. His condition is still serious, but he's a strong man and his vital signs are good. We were able to repair his leg. Most of his ribs were broken, but none punctured a lung. His heart took a blow from the impact of that horse falling on him—the shock and pressure were intense—but he's going to be all right. He's really a very lucky man."

"When can we see him?"

"Go talk to the charge nurse and see if he's awake. You girls can go visit him if he is, but make sure not to stay too long. And don't be surprised if he is not very responsive. He should be pretty groggy from the surgery. Remember that rest is our biggest ally right now."

Elizabeth and Kyle stood up. "Just the girls for now," he repeated, looking at Arthur and Esther. "And of course his wife when she arrives. Come girls, follow me."

At the door of their father's room, Elizabeth's hands began to shake, and Kyle's eyes darted around the room at all the strange equipment surrounding her father. Machines hummed persistently. Was the person in the bed their tall, take-charge dad? Kyle took a deep breath and slowly approached him. "Dad?" she whispered tentatively.

"You can talk a little louder, honey," said the nurse who was adjusting one of the tubes. "It's okay to let him know you're here."

She spoke a little louder and gently took his hand, giving it a tiny squeeze. "I love you, Daddy." Elizabeth went next. She was more forceful than her sister and had no trouble speaking up, but the experience was unnerving. She had never seen her father this way. Would he ever be the same again? He stirred briefly, opening his eyes just long enough to give the girls a tender smile. The girls watched him as he drifted back to sleep before they left the room.

Slowly they made their way back to Arthur and Esther, wondering what to do next and grateful when Esther suggested breakfast. The cafeteria was bustling. Esther gently urged them to eat something substantial. She was curious to hear their reactions to seeing their father, but she knew they would speak when they were ready. Elizabeth and Kyle did look up and say, "Thank you guys for being here," before looking down again, unable to say more.

Time seemed locked in some alien universe, and they didn't know what to do except what they were doing. Their reverie was interrupted by a cheerful male nurse, inquiring if either of the girls was an Elizabeth or a Kyle Litchfield. "You have a telephone call."

"Maybe it's mom! Let's go."

Mindy was on the line. "Hi, any news of your dad this morning?"

They gave her the latest report. "Where is Mom? Is she coming home? Does she need a ride or anything?"

"She's on her way, but I'm afraid there's been some trouble at the house. In a nutshell, there was a burglary and the police are here. You might want to come to the house if you can."

"Were you in the house when it happened? Is everything all right?"

"No…no…I came after it happened. We'll know more when your mom gets here and a report is made. I'll see you soon, then?"

Elizabeth relayed Mindy's message, her face pale with shock. "Oh, Esther, what if we had been there? We could have gotten hurt!"

"Boy, when it rains, it pours, doesn't it? I hope whoever did it didn't get in the safe. Tori has such lovely things in there. I think your mom has a special story for each piece."

"Arthur?"

"Let's go."

Chapter 5

"*Sempre bellisima*, Tori. Always beautiful! Did you see John Fairchild smiling? That man is a notorious grouch. If he liked it, then everyone will. You'll see. We will be in *Women's Wear Daily* tomorrow."

Tori smiled. Luca was her one-man cheering squad, as he had always been. They first met in design school where a class project brought them together, and they had been fast friends ever since. Later when she started her own business, she called Luca and asked if he'd come work for her. He jumped at the chance. Not only was he very fond of her, he also recognized her talent and knew this was his chance to advance in the competitive world of fashion photography.

Now they sat enjoying the usual rehash of the show. It was part gossip, part professional critique. This post-game dialogue with Luca was a treasured interlude that gave them both a chance to unwind before the beginning of a new project.

Vogue had promised her a spread in an early spring issue, and no expense had been spared to assure the highest quality photos. They had chosen Malta from pictures of its exotic ruins and turquoise waters. The collection, she felt, would reestablish her reputation on 7th avenue. It was not often that designers were given a second chance, and she wanted to prove to the fashion industry that they had been right in welcoming her back after her hiatus.

Tori turned as she heard approaching footsteps. It was Mindy. "Need anything else before I head out in the morning to pick up the jewelry from your house?"

"I don't think so, Mindy. Just get the jewelry. You've taken care of all the trip details, and Luca is going to meet us at the airport."

"Okay. By the way, did you return Esther's call?"

"Oops, no, I didn't. Was that Esther who called? I'll do it as soon as I get to the hotel this evening."

"It was an emergency, Tori. Please call as soon as you are able. I don't want them to think that I forgot to tell you. I'll talk to you tomorrow after I pick up the jewelry, in case there is anything else you want me to bring."

"Good girl, Mindy. Drive safely. The leaves are just blazing now. It should be a splendid ride."

"I'll leave with you. Ciao, Tori," and Luca and Mindy were out the door.

Tori sat quietly breathing in the success of the show a bit longer before gathering up her jacket and purse. At the door she hesitated but quickly reassured herself that she had done a full day's work and needed rest. She shut off the lights, locked the large door to the loft, and headed for the sidewalk to hail a cab. She gave the driver the name of her hotel and leaned back against the worn black leather seat, closing her eyes and trusting him to maneuver the late night traffic. Jolted awake as he pulled up to the hotel entrance, she leaned forward to stuff some bills into his hand through the partition. Half asleep, she acknowledged the doorman with a faint smile, entered the elevator, and headed straight to her room.

Shedding her clothes, she wrapped herself in her favorite silk robe and went through her nightly routine of creams and lotions. No matter how tired she was, she never would forego this ritual. Her creamy complexion was part of her trademark, and she adored the attention it brought her. As she turned down the covers from the bed, she realized she hadn't eaten all day, which was not that unusual for her on the day of a show. She was suddenly ravenous but too tired to wait for room service. Instead, she found some cookies on top of the TV and munched those. Crawling between the sheets, she remembered that she had still not returned Esther's call. "Oh, dear! I'll do it first thing in the morning. She'll understand." She muttered groggily to herself, *I'm so tired, so tired,* and was asleep as soon as the lights were off.

Chapter 6

THE phone began to ring. Tori stirred restlessly and pulled the covers around her head, shutting out the light coming through the draperies, but not shutting out the sound coming from beside her bed. She sat up and reached for the phone.

"Hello?"

The voice on the other end sounded concerned. "Tori?"

"Is this Mindy?"

"Yes… Something strange is going on at your house. The front door is open and no one seems to be in the house!"

"Are you sure? Have you gone in?"

"No, I was afraid to. At first, I thought maybe the girls had come by, but they're still at the hospital. I checked."

"Hospital? What happened to them?"

"Nothing happened to *them*. Didn't you return Esther's call?"

"No, I fell asleep. Sorry."

"Oh, Tori, then you don't know! David was in an accident. He's at St. Elizabeth. "Well, Mindy, you had better call the police if the house looks suspicious. It might be a burglary. And don't go inside in case someone is still there. I'll leave the city just as soon as I get dressed."

Tori put down the phone and sprang to her feet, her heart racing. Instantly awake, she surveyed the disorder of the night before. Clothes were strewn over the chairs, and wrappers from the cookies lay on the floor. She made her way to the bathroom, washed her face and brushed her teeth, and got dressed.

David is in the hospital…an accident? Whatever could have happened? He is a good driver…but maybe someone ran a stop sign, or lost control on a curve, or—who knows? Well, if he's at St. Elizabeth's, then he's in good hands. I'm sure he'll be okay. Oh God, please let it be nothing serious.

Tori grabbed her purse and weekend bag and took the elevator straight down to the garage. Her silver Jaguar was soon careening up 7th avenue and toward the Lincoln Tunnel. Her anxiety rising, she pressed harder on the gas pedal. By the time she was out of the city, she was practically flying.

The ride which normally took two hours she drove in ninety minutes. She was almost hysterical when she arrived.

Tori hardly recognized her driveway filled with the flashing lights of several emergency vehicles. She sat for a moment after turning off the engine, simply taking in the scene and gathering her thoughts. Elizabeth and Kyle ran toward the car and pulled open the door. "Mom, come, hurry! There's been a burglary, and did you hear about Dad? Oh Mom, why didn't you call?"

"Oh girls, I was just so tired, I was running on empty. I didn't know the call was a real emergency. These big shows always wipe me out, and when I got back to the hotel, I just fell into bed. I'm sorry I didn't get back to you. How is your father?"

"He's going to be okay, Mom, but he nearly died," Elizabeth said, her voice cracking. "They moved him out of ICU and into a private room this morning, but's it's still serious. His leg was really messed up and most of his ribs were broken, and I think his back is pretty bad, too. Plus, Mom, his heart stopped! Just for a few minutes when he was on his way to the hospital……but, anyway, the doctor said he is very lucky to survive. A horse fell on him, Mom!"

"What on earth was he doing?"

Esther stepped up and threw her arms around Tori. Pulling back, she explained, "It's my fault, Tori. Breeze threw him off and fell on top of him. I feel so responsible. The horse was startled by a truck backfiring."

"Mom, Mom, can we go to the hospital now?"

"I want to go, girls, but I've got to take care of this first. Where's Mindy?"

Mindy appeared immediately at her side. "The police wouldn't let me in until you got here, but they said we could go in now."

Tori could hardly believe her eyes. She ran quickly around the room, looking through the disheveled open drawers. She felt invaded. Whoever it was had obviously rummaged through them as well as the closets, clearing the tops of dressers with no mercy. They even took the safe. Nothing was left, not even the costume jewelry. She sat down on the bed and tried to pull herself together. Her mind catalogued each piece and the story that went with each. Memories were all she had now of her most exquisite jewels. Tears threatened to overflow, but she quickly pushed them away and stood up.

"Mindy, we need *something* for the shoot. Call people, do whatever you need to do, but we need some jewelry. I have to give a statement to the police now, so I'll go down and do that. Then I must go see David. Let me know when you have found something."

Interlude, Jewels of the Heart

Muktananda, my wise baba, once told me that a gift was on its way to me and would arrive in just a few weeks. I awaited the gift with anticipation and excitement. Never could I have imagined that in a few weeks all of my priceless jewelry would be stolen. A gift? Was this a joke? How the loss of my cherished treasures was a gift took some time for me to understand. The list was long: The 9 mm pearls from Japan and bracelet left on my dresser, along with a 15-caret heart-shaped amethyst and omega necklace; a turquoise and gold bracelet, some jade and gold earrings, an exquisite handmade Cabashon emerald ring with tiny rosebuds—all probably sold for a song. They were all beautiful and expensive, but more importantly they carried deep sentimental value, such as the diamond bracelet David gave me in honor of becoming a grandmother. Only bittersweet memories remained.

And what do I think now? In this time we have here on earth, all is for the giving and taking. Everything is impermanent, granted to us only temporarily. What we keep is our connection to God, to the One Consciousness. That is the gift I received when I lost many of the things I thought were valuable in my life. That lesson was priceless. Thank you, Baba.

Chapter 7

THE usual hush in the hospital corridors was interrupted by voices carrying an air of lightness and frivolity. Tori wondered why it annoyed her so. It seemed rude in such a serious setting. As she and the girls approached David's room in silence, they passed an open door through which they saw an older gentleman in a wheelchair. He was surrounded by what appeared to be numerous friends and relatives all laughing and talking. They were not speaking English, but Tori could tell they were enjoying each other's company. There were so many visitors that a small knot had overflowed into the hallway. Among those was a woman elegantly dressed in a tailored peach-colored suit and a white wide-brimmed hat who paused and turned as Tori and the girls approached. "Beatrici, Matteo, please, allow Mrs. Litchfield to pass by." Tori managed a feeble smile in appreciation of the courtesy.

"Hey, Mom, that lady knows your name. Who is she? Do you know her?" Kyle whispered.

"No, I don't know her. I have never seen any of them before. But I suppose one needn't be a genius to figure it out!" She affected a smile as she tapped at the nameplate beside her husband's room. "You two stay out here for a few minutes while I see your father alone, all right?"

Tori pushed open the door and found David barely able to open his eyes to greet her. Obviously the noise which was such an annoyance to her from next door had no effect on his ability to sleep. Tori leaned over and kissed him on his forehead. "Oh my, how awful this is. Sweetheart, how are you feeling?" Before he could even attempt an answer, she had moved away from his side and began fussing with the curtains in the room. She looked outside to see if he had a view and made a note to have Mindy send some flowers. She was obviously distracted as she began talking half to herself, "I don't know if the girls told you, but there was a thief at the house who took all my jewelry. It's quite a mess. I don't know what I am going to do. I have a flight scheduled for Malta tomorrow—I think I told you that—to do a photo shoot, and now I have no jewelry for my models to wear."

Crossing back to the bed, she took his hand. It tugged at her heart to see David looking so helpless and hooked up to all the machines. She felt conflicted about leaving him. Was she being selfish? This was her husband lying here. She had a responsibility to him, but this opportunity with *Vogue* was a 'once in a lifetime' chance; and if they rescheduled the shoot, the costs would be exorbitant. She was interrupted by a messenger from the nurse's station. "Mrs. Litchfield, you have a message from your assistant, Mindy—something about having found some jewelry? She needs your signature for the insurance."

"You're in good hands, sweetheart," she whispered to him. "You're strong as an ox. I've got to go now and take care of some things before I jump on the plane." She squeezed his hand briefly. "I do love you," she said as her eyes searched his face. "See you soon. I'll be back before you miss me."

Tori opened her arms to embrace the girls as she hastily exited the room. "Be brave girls and take care of your dad for me while I'm gone. I love you two."

"Where are you going, Mom?"

"Mindy called and found some jewelry I can use for the shoot. I've got to go."

"Oh, Mom! No! Right this second?"

"Yes, I'll call you. Don't worry. Esther will help you two!" and with flying kisses she turned and nearly crashed directly into Esther.

"You are leaving, Tori?"

"Yes. I must. I'll call you. We'll be in Malta Monday afternoon. Thank you, Esther," in a softer voice, "and Arthur, too, for all you two have done here. Where would we be without you?"

Turning away and flying down the hall, she waved her fingers behind her and called, "Bye, bye, I'll be back before you miss me."

Esther's gaze followed Tori until she passed out of sight. With a sigh, she turned to catch the eye of the woman with the wide-brimmed hat now engaged in conversation with the girls. They had introduced themselves and asked her what language she was speaking. As Esther walked toward them, she overheard the woman say, "My name is Gabriella, and we are all from Malta. Your mother will love it there. It will change her, forever. It is a very special place, filled with real magic."

Interlude, Early Rejection

I know by now you must think I am a terrible person, even a terrible mother. I just did the best I knew how. It took me a long time to come to terms with my life, with the damages that had been wrought, and then learn how to repair them.

What I knew of love was mostly duty. It started with my mother's rejection of me when my brother was born. I was six years old. Daddy woke me in the middle of the night and said it was time for Mommy to go to the hospital to have my brother. On the way, he dropped me at my Aunt Dorie's and Uncle Shep's house, which I had always loved to visit. Two weeks passed before they came to get me. I had missed them so much and was very excited to meet my new brother. I went into the house, hung up my coat, and climbed the stairs, trying not to make noise. Daddy told me the baby and Mommy might be sleeping. I entered the room that Daddy had said Mommy and the baby would be in and remember looking around. The beds and night tables were in the same place, as were the dressers, dressing table, and chairs. All was just as I had left it. All was in order.

Mommy was in the rocking chair, looking down at the baby. I stood there, hardly able to breathe, waiting, waiting. I whispered, "I missed you, Mommy." I walked closer. Mommy never moved. There was only silence. I waited another minute and walked out of the room.

I said to myself, 'I'm outa here.' At six I left my body, and it took many years to walk back into it. I played the role of a needy, needy child for a long time: needing love from others, needing friendship, needing things to collect for posterity, needing stuff to show my worth. This life found itself eventually opening to rebirth, having been nurtured first in a cave of darkness. I had separated from myself as I hid playing the role of a character I created one day at a time. Who was I? It depended on the time, it depended on the circumstances. Let me tell you, it took me a long time to emerge from that cave; but I did it, one step at a time, and have only gratitude for this life and for the love along the way, always the love.

Chapter 8

AFTER a long restless flight from New York to Rome, Tori and her small entourage exited the airplane into Fiumicino-Leonardo da Vinci airport. It was a short stopover before their connecting flight to Malta, and with Luca's help they quickly ordered a cafè lattè and almond biscotti.

"It feels so good to stretch our legs, doesn't it?" Tori walked back and forth a few times in front of their small table before she settled into her chair. Her mind was filled with details that still needed to be worked out, and she was impatient to get them settled. She did her best thinking standing up.

"Mindy, have you arranged for a van and drivers to takes us to and from the sites and a few local boys to help Luca with the setup?"

"It is all done, Tori. Not to worry. Luca made a few calls. He has some friends who are coming to help us out."

Tori smiled; she was impressed. She always could rely on Mindy to get everything prepared down to the last detail. She was surprised, though, that Luca had friends in Malta.

"Have you been here before, Luca?"

"I've traveled a lot in my life," he said after a short pause.

She was about to ask another question when Mindy broke in. "I checked with the hotel, and all our rooms are ready. Plus, they offer yummy picnic lunches of fresh pesto and focaccia, so that takes care of the food! And don't forget to call David and the girls..." Mindy stopped as she saw some annoyance on Tori's face. Perhaps she had overstepped her boundary.

"Of course I will remember… yes… the girls…and yes, David, too. Of course I will," her tone running the gambit of agreeable to irritated. Luca held up his hand to silence the women as Mindy began to voice an apology. He wanted to listen to the announcement for their connecting flight which was made first in Italian, and then in English.

Deplaning at Luqa airport in Malta, the light exploded around them. It was a perfect Mediterranean afternoon, the sea in the distance full of sparkling waves and boats of red, blue, and yellow—the traditional colors of Malta. Tori had never seen anything quite so beautiful, and she considered herself a seasoned traveler. Glancing toward Luca for a silent confirmation of the exquisite light and beauty, she caught a hint of melancholy in his face. She studied him as he took an intentionally deep breath and with effort gave a big smile.

"What do you think, Tori? Is this not the perfect location for your designs?" There was no trace whatsoever of the emotion from before, either in his tone or on his face; and as her mind quickly jumped ahead to the next day's shoot, she tried to make a mental note to question him about this.

Dawn the following morning was equally as spectacular as the previous afternoon. The air was magical; and Tori was happy, excited, and definitely in the flow, her focus undivided. The shoot was effortless. Music, courtesy of a group of locals, serenaded them all afternoon. Flutes and guitars reminiscent of Turkish folk music enlivened the air, and the models worked effortlessly. The girls remained fresh and energetic even after long hours in the sun and breeze, and Luca cajoled and charmed them into beautiful shots. As evening approached and the final shots of the day were being set up, the long trip combined with the recent events in New York—the show, David's accident, and the burglary finally began to take their toll on Tori. When she snapped at a particular model for the third time, Luca took her aside.

"Tori, we have had a fantastic day. It's been very long, and you are very tired. Let's not ruin everything now. Please, you go back to the hotel and have a drink and watch the sunset. I have only a few more shots and a few more minutes to catch the light. You go ahead and I will meet you."

To everyone's surprise, she agreed.

At the café nearest their hotel in Valetta Tori plunked herself down and ordered a glass of wine. It was lovely to relax, she had to admit. The café opened to the sidewalk, and a light sea breeze carried a tang that teased the senses. She admired the imposing houses of classical design overlooking the harbor and stared dreamily into the sunset. It was not until a woman's greeting from the next table was repeated for the second time that her reverie was broken. Tori turned toward a woman wearing a stunning yet simple yellow dress with matching sweater adorned with pearl buttons. She recognized the designer, a popular Italian she had met in New York last season. The woman carried the clearly expensive design beautifully with no hint of personal display, just an aura of someone who was comfortable in her own skin. Tori wondered if someday she could affect that same aura. The quiet self-confidence that she saw had always eluded her.

"I am Gabriella," the woman said, graciously offering her hand.

"I'm Victoria......Tori."

"Yes. Are you enjoying your stay in Malta?" The voice had a familiar ring, but she couldn't place it. The accent was soothing and invited conversation.

"I'm here to work and yes, I am enjoying it. It is an exquisitely beautiful country. I really didn't know what to expect, but it's *very* beautiful. I am doing a fashion shoot for *Vogue,* and it is going well. I love your outfit!"

Tori could take up a conversation with anyone as long as she could keep it superficial. She was not one to share much of her personal life, but she was a good conversationalist and enjoyed meeting new people. She soon found herself chatting away about fashion and her new designs.

"I can't help but notice the beautiful outfit you have on. I love the drape of the hem. He does such good work, doesn't he?"

"Do you know him?"

"Mostly by his work, but I have met him a time or two at shows."

Just as she was about to say something else, Tori spotted Luca hurrying toward them. "Gabriella, this is Luca, my photographer," she turned to introduce Gabriella to Luca and missed the look that passed between them.

"Won't you join us for a drink, Luca?"

"Of course! My pleasure! I'll go place an order."

Tori watched as Luca went off and spoke to the waiter. What language was he speaking now? It didn't sound like Italian. Was it Maltese? How did he know Maltese?

She turned toward Gabriella to ask her to verify his speech when the woman launched into a history of the island. "It predates places such as Stonehenge and the Pyramids, before the great masters such as Buddha, Mohammed, Moses, Jesus. The religion here was centered on the goddess and emphasized equality between the sexes. There was a reverence for nature, and an understanding of women's fertility and creation as being very like that of the earth itself. Malta is very proud of its 1,500-year history of peace; and most interesting, no artifacts of war have ever been unearthed by archaeologists! Artifacts determined to be 6,000 years old have been discovered, but none related to war. You will see. The peace of our country permeates the rocks themselves!"

"That's a lovely story," Tori commented as Luca returned to the table. The waiter followed with appetizers for them to try.

"Thanks for ordering those, Luca. The olives look particularly wonderful. What kind of cheese is that? And Luca, I didn't know you could speak Maltese. Were you speaking Maltese?"

"It's a special feta cheese made here on the island. Try the hummus too, Tori, you will love it!"

"If you're interested, Tori," Gabriella gently touched her arm, "*I'd* like to take you somewhere special this evening to see the Sleeping Lady. It's a sculpture that represents the goddess religion I was telling you about. There is a ceremony in the Hypogeum not far from your hotel. I am sure you will find it interesting, and I would be very pleased if you would accompany me." Tori ignored the arguments arising in her head, sipped her wine, and made a promise to herself to stop and just surrender to the magic of the evening and the island. All her questions could be answered later.

Chapter 9

The wooden balcony was the perfect spot to view the full moon rising and breathe in the fragrance of geraniums wafting from the flower-filled balconies along the cobbled streets. Tori studied the hotel brochure which explained the history of Malta and its capital city of Valletta. She wished she had time to explore more of the island and was happy that she had accepted Gabriella's offer to visit the Hypogeum that evening. Someday she would come back as a tourist to take in the other sites. It wouldn't be this trip, as their schedule was completely filled, and she had to get back to David as soon as possible. She was especially interested in seeing St. John's Catholic Church with its austere looking fortress façade and its interior filled with priceless art from the Baroque era. The Knights of Malta, noblemen from the most important families of Europe, had commissioned the construction of the church and their new city after defending their tiny island from the Ottomans. The Knights had turned Malta into a fortress that 'befitted a military Order and built a new capital city worthy of noblemen'. St. John's was the gem of their generous donations. Yes, she would have to come back. Perhaps with David and the girls.

The day's accumulation of hurry and exhaustion melted away, and Tori was looking forward to her meeting with Gabriella. She had a second wind. It would be an adventure, and this island seemed uniquely full of history, mystery and adventure. From the balcony, Tori could see Gabriella's sleek black Fiat draw up to the entrance of the hotel. She called down to her and smiled graciously as the doorman assisted her into the car. She turned to greet her new friend.

"Hello, Gabriella!"

"Hello, Tori. I see that you are dressed appropriately for the occasion. You'll be glad you have that wrap, and those flat shoes will make it easier to get up and down the stairs into the Hypogeum."

"Yes. I discovered that these streets, though quaint, don't make for easy walking. I nearly turned my ankle the first day. I noticed that the locals never wear high heels, and from my other travels I have discovered that 'to do as in Rome' just makes life easier. It's lovely to see you, Gabriella. I wasn't sure if I really had time for this this evening. "

"Well, I am very happy you decided to come, Tori. I think this will be very important for you, especially with all that's going on in your life. You are always where you are supposed to be. You have been preparing for this for a long time; very soon all of this will become clear."

Gabriella had such a charming way of speaking with such intimacy and sincerity that Tori decided it would be rude to question the content of that statement. Instead she focused on staying alive as they whizzed through the narrow streets toward Paola. The local mantra was 'drive it like it's stolen!' and this divinely poised woman deftly maneuvering the streets had definitely gotten that memo!

Paola was the village where the 5,000-year-old ruin, the Hypogeum, and its famous Sleeping Goddess was located. Hypogeum means 'underground' in Greek, and Tori would soon accompany Gabriella three stories beneath the surface into the only *prehistoric* underground temple in the world! When archaeologists discovered the Hypogeum, they originally thought it was a burial chamber, and perhaps it had been; but it was also a sacred place used for ceremonies during the time of the goddess, just as it was going to be used tonight.

As they started to descend the stairs, Tori prayed that her occasional claustrophobia would not be a problem. Ten meters below the street was the first level, an elaborate necropolis from prehistoric times. She was acutely aware of a sudden change in atmosphere, and not just because it was cooler and quieter! Continuing down into the main room, a roughly circular chamber, Tori stopped to let her eyes adjust to the dimly lit space. Gabriella smiled reassuringly and slipped her arm through Tori's as she led her toward the entrance to the Oracle room, a rectangular room with a painted ceiling of circles and spirals. Gabriella had chosen this spot for them, knowing that the exceptional acoustics of this room would be a treat for Tori to hear once the singing started.

The main room soon became crowded with women of many different ages and nationalities, all reverentially silent. Tori had, of course, been in temples and churches in her travels, but this space had a unique energy that sent chills up and down her spine. It was then that she caught sight of the Sleeping Lady who was resting on her arm napping, or as Gabriella told her, 'incubating.' The voluptuous figure was a mere six inches long but held a surprisingly powerful attraction for Tori. Flooded by sensations, she drew her shawl closer, feeling overwhelmed with gratitude and nostalgia. Oh, how she missed David and her girls. She smiled softly towards Gabriella who drew closer as the singing started. It wasn't hard to join in with the tune, and the acoustics in the room *were* out of this world—better than in any concert hall she had been in. The women swayed and sang, moving gently and effortlessly in a spontaneously choreographed expression of union and love. Tori, much to her surprise, found herself caught up in the spirit of the moment, freely enjoying the strong power and presence of this feminine energy. It fascinated her. When they were done, there was a prayer to the Sleeping Lady asking for her blessing, the candles were extinguished, and then complete silence. A sliver of moonlight that had entered the room from above helped guide them back up the stairs.

It had been more than Tori could have expected, and she was somewhat speechless. Gabriella was the first to break the silence as they walked toward the car.

"I just wanted to expose you to this tonight. I think this will be important to you, to know that the world was not always patriarchal."

"I've never been to anything like this, and the feeling of sharing this with other women was amazing to me. I feel a bit sad…and happy, but I can't really talk about it coherently right now."

"There is time. Not to worry. We will talk later," Gabriella assured her. At the hotel Gabriella kissed Tori on either cheek, wishing her all the best with the rest of her stay in Malta. Tori felt like she was leaving a dear and close friend and again felt a rush of deep emotion surge through her body. She waited as Gabriella sped away from the hotel and then headed for her room. Her dreams that night were filled with images from the Hypogeum. It felt like a door was opening for her into a world once lived thousands and thousands of years ago. She slept like she hadn't for years-- a deep and completely refreshing sleep.

Interlude, Rumi Poem

The breeze at dawn has secrets to tell you;
Don't go back to sleep.

You must ask for what you really want.
Don't go back to sleep.

People are going back and forth across the
door sill
where the two worlds touch.

The door is round and open.
Don't go back to sleep.

-Rumi

Chapter 10

Tori and Luca were the only ones from their party in the hotel dining room for breakfast. Shore birds had just begun flying over the sparkling water, their cries for food shrill above the gently lapping waves. Sunrise had always been a special time for Tori; *hope springs eternal* was the phrase that best described her optimism with the returning light. She met each day with the anticipation of possibility.

Coffee cup in hand, she stood up and invited Luca to join her on a stroll down to the pier to feed the birds. He grabbed several pieces of hot bread from the basket on the table and followed Tori, surprised at her easeful demeanor which was quite the contrast to her studio 'persona'.

"Want a taste before I feed them?" He held it up to her mouth, close enough for her to take a bite. She steadied his hand as she sampled the bread. After drawing a shaky breath, she said, "I always wonder who is on those boats and where they are going."

"Mmmm," was his reply. They were quiet then and watched the sunlight spread over the water and illuminate the buildings behind them, turning the old walls into edifices of gold. Luca threw the last few crumbs to the circling gulls, and without a word they made their way back to the dining room.

By now everyone in their party was there, still a bit sleepy but excited about the day's adventure. They were taking a trip to Gozo, and Mindy was giving the crew a short history of the famous Ggantija temples. "They are around 5,800 years old and dedicated to the Great Earth Mother. In the past there was an oracle, a priestess possessed of the spirit of the goddess. It was a place to pray for healing, as well." Tori smiled, thinking about her experiences of the night before and wondering if she could explain to them how magical it had been. Maybe she would try on the plane trip home.

Gozo, an even smaller island than Malta, was a quick 20-minute ferry ride north. Luca teased that it would be an invigorating swim and threatened to throw one of the models overboard! Luca turned toward Tori, expecting a reprimanding stare and surprisingly was greeted with a big smile. Everyone noticed the lightness in mood, and it was contagious. Debarking from the ferry they discovered Gozo to be greener and lusher than Malta, dense with oleander, geraniums, and bougainvillea spilling over the round, curved buildings. No matter where one walked, the sea was only a stone's throw away. Enchanted by the landscape, the girls gave a different energy to what they were doing, feeling like goddesses themselves from an ancient time as they modeled on the temple steps.

The morning passed quickly. After breaking for lunch in a little café, they finished their work and were back on the ferry by mid-afternoon. The mood on the way back to Valetta was happy yet subdued, as Luca and Tori and the rest of the crew gazed out over the sea, clear turquoise today with crystal waves under a cloudless sky. Tori saw that the others were feeling that same gratitude mixed with nostalgia she had been feeling since the night before. It had been a beautiful trip, more so than she had even imagined.

That night the crew had dinner together. There was lots of wine, lots of seafood and pasta, lots of laughing. Somewhere in the night they heard singing and went out into the streets to find it. There was a small band of local musicians, and soon they were dancing with abandon. They gave themselves to the enchantment of the night lit by a nearly full moon. Finally weary from the long day, they crossed back to the hotel wishing each other *sweet dreams* in whispers that echoed faintly in the night.

Chapter 11

Luca was feeling restless, and after bidding everyone a 'good night' he headed for a drink and maybe some food. There were still quite a few revelers in the bar as he made his way to the counter and ordered some wine. Glass in hand, he turned to find a place to sit down, when he heard someone call his name.

"Hey Luca! What are you doing here?"

He turned sharply, nearly spilling his wine.

"Over here, close to the door!"

He pushed through the crowd and found his friend Sean sitting at a table by himself. Sean stood up, and he and Luca had a pounding embrace, thumping each other on the back.

"Well my friend, you are the last person I thought I'd see here. What brings you to Malta?" Luca could hardly believe his luck. He hadn't seen Sean for a long time, not since he had stopped acting and decided to become a photo-journalist."I could ask you the same thing, buddy, but I'm assuming you came home to see your family. How are they?"

Luca shifted uncomfortably. "I don't know. I haven't called them. I'm working for a fashion designer in New York, and we're here doing a photo shoot. No one from my family knows I'm here. Don't blow my cover! We leave tomorrow. Anyway, what are you up to?"

"I'll tell you that in a minute, but is there something wrong? I thought you and your family were close."

"Not so much anymore. I respect what they're doing, but I'm just not interested in being a part of it. I really love my job, and the woman I work with is on the fast track. It's great for my career, and we work together really well. Besides, it's New York! What can I say?"

"Well, Luca, I can't argue with you. Tell me more about this woman! Is anything going on there?" Sean grinned mischievously.

"It's just work, I'm afraid. She's married."

"Happily?"

Luca laughed. "I suppose. Her husband is a business guy, brilliant, a wheeler-dealer. You know the type. She's pretty focused on her work, driven actually. I have to tell you though, Sean, she's beautiful."

"Speaking of what the world throws at you, I assume you're pretty much up on what's going on in 'Nam? You'd have to be living under a rock not to be. It's all such a mess, and we're not getting the real truth of what's happening. I'm leaving to go there day after tomorrow."

Luca interrupted before he could say more. "Sean! Wait a minute! You're going to Vietnam voluntarily?"

"They're not telling us what's really happening…the government, the politicians, and the big military-industrial complex that's making money off this thing. There are too many people dying, Luca, and for what?"

"So you want to go and find out?"

"Yah, I do. And I want *you* to come with me; it might do you good!! Not that this'll be any kind of vacation, but together we could get some killer pictures and maybe even change foreign policy. I could really use some help, and man, you're one of the best."

"Vietnam! You've got to be kidding, Sean. That sounds ridiculous, not to mention dangerous. I'm a fashion photographer, for God's sake."

"Are you ready for another drink? Let's grab one, and maybe a handful of whatever they have to munch on here and go out on the pier and talk. This is no place to have a real conversation."

The pier was quiet, and they found a place to sit where they could see the water. The moon traveled across the sky as they talked. They spoke of their duty to themselves, to others, to their country to use the talents they possessed for some meaningful purpose. Caught up in the fast world of fashion design in New York, Luca had not spent much time thinking about his deeper purpose. He was just too busy. Quiet nights and deep talks like this were too few and far between. He realized that the questions of *who am I* and *why am I here* had gone unanswered for some time. Maybe it *was* time.

In the end, surprising himself, Luca agreed to join Sean for a month. "I don't think it was a coincidence that we ran into each other tonight, Sean."

"No, it wasn't. I believe in synchronicity, and I try to pay attention when it comes across my path."

"There's just one condition. I need to be back in New York in a month. The photos for the spring layout in Vogue are due, and I have obligations there. Maybe they're not as important or exciting as what we're about to do, but I am loyal—to my job and to Tori."

"That's fair. Right on, brother. I'll have ya back in a month…scout's honor."

They shook hands as they stood up in the early hours of the morning, realizing, without saying the words, that they were forging a bond neither had envisioned. They embraced again and parted. Inspired by purpose, Luca strode energetically across the smooth stones and then walked as quietly as he could to his room, nodding conspiratorially to the doorman as he tiptoed through the lobby. The doorman winked, thinking his arrival in the wee hours had to do with some woman. And in a way, it did. He fell asleep wondering how he was going to tell Tori that he wouldn't be going back to New York.

Chapter 12

TORI was awake at first light. Had last night been a dream? She couldn't remember the last time when she had felt so free, so happy. She had slept the whole night through without waking. Was it Malta…..the success of the shoot? Luca? She tried to push the last out of her mind, but it was impossible. Their professional relationship had always felt completely *simpatico*, but there clearly was more. However, what the "more" was defied easy explanation. *Do I really need to complicate my life this way?* Well, she would deal with it later.

Her wake-up call found her ready to get going, and she rose with arms outstretched as if she were embracing the city itself. One more shoot this morning, and then they would be done and on the evening flight back to Rome.

The dining hall was a bit more crowded today. Others were up early, probably to take advantage of their last day, too. Breakfast was good, as always, and the coffee hot and strong.

Today Luca was taking some shots of the models with more of the city in the background. The sea was always such a temptation, but he felt that having more of the city featured was a good idea. The crew chattered among themselves while everything was made ready. It seemed that the gods, or the goddesses, surely were smiling on them all. The air seemed to sparkle, the breeze was light, and the scent of bread baking in one of the little houses nearby tempted them from across the stones.

Tori was in top form today; and although her eyes were everywhere noticing details that no one else saw, her direction was softened. These were her designs. She knew how she wanted them presented; she knew the kind of statement she wanted to make. 'The devil is in the details.' She knew what it took to make the whole outfit shine.

"Have you finished packing, Tori?"

"I just have a few more things to finish up, and I want to call home again before I leave. I did leave a number where the hospital could reach me, but I haven't heard from them. If I don't get through to them this time, I may just have to wait 'til I get to New York. Anyway, after that's done, I want to have one more glass of wine in that delightful little café. The plane doesn't leave for Rome until 5:00 p.m. How about you? Are you ready?"

He bent down to pick up his tripod and cameras. "I'll join you for wine, if I may. There are some things we need to talk about. See you about three?"

"I thought the shoot went really well, didn't you? I can't wait to see it all laid out. The way you and the models were working together was just like watching a dance, complete with fabulous costumes. I was impressed!"

"Good. That's the way it should be when it's all in sync. Mother nature was smiling on us this week. See you at three."

Luca went to his room to store his equipment. His skin prickled with excitement and trepidation. What was he getting himself into? He really wasn't an impetuous person; and he liked to plan his moves carefully, to calculate his chances with things. It had been a long time since he had taken such a big risk—not since he decided to leave Malta for New York. Trust, maybe that was what this was all about; that, and a willingness to stretch and go beyond comfortable boundaries. He took a deep breath as he checked his collar in the mirror, exhaled, and went downstairs to tell Tori of his plans.

She was already seated. His heart flip-flopped as he caught her eye.

"You started without me, I see?" Catching the eye of the waiter, he pointed to the glass and soon had his own drink to sip.

"Tori." "Luca." They both spoke at the same time.

"You go first," she ceded.

"Okay. What I have to say is hard, and there's no way to sugar coat it. I'm not going back to New York right now."

"You're what? But….why? I would love to stay, too. This is such a beautiful place. But I have to get back for the girls…and David."

"No, Tori. It is not what you think. It is not for … I'm going to Vietnam."

"What! Why? When? Are you crazy? We have the layout!"

He held up his hand. "Hear me out." He told her about his meeting with Sean the previous evening, their all-night discussion, and his decision. "I don't know if I can explain this completely, Tori. I know it all sounds a little crazy, and maybe it is. I have decided it is something I have to do. But listen, I'm not abandoning you. I'll be back in a month, and then it's back to work. I can look over the film while I'm gone and send the photographs to New York. I promise!"

"Oh Luca, I don't know what to say. I don't know what I'll do without you."

The café was quiet in mid-afternoon. The Mediterranean siesta meant that many people were resting in their rooms, their homes, or their boats. Only a single woman occupied a small table in the back. Her broad-brimmed hat shaded her face, and her dress fell softly around her shoulders as she watched the pair. Intent on each other, they never noticed her presence. Her heart opened to them, knowing all too well their journey ahead.

Chapter 13

Elizabeth sat by her dad's bedside while her sister went to their mom's favorite florist to get the flowers they had ordered. The shop would have delivered, but Kyle knew the proprietor would want a first-hand report on David. Elizabeth focused on her father's face, which looked brighter and more relaxed than it had two days ago. The doctor was right. Her dad was strong and would heal with time and rest, and with all the prayers being sent his way.

"Good morning, Dad."

"Hi, sweetie. How are you? Are you getting any rest? You and Kyle seem to be here pretty much round the clock. Every time I come to, it seems like you both are at the ready."

"We're fine. We're young, remember, and strong like you. I'm just so glad you're feeling better."

"I am. Have you heard from Mom?"

"She tried to call when she landed in Malta; but there was so much static on the line, all we could manage was 'hello' and her signature 'I'll be back before you miss me!' So we haven't really had a conversation."

"I'm sure she'll call again."

Elizabeth wasn't so sure; she knew how obsessed with work her mom could be, plus juggling time zones would be difficult for her.

Just then Kyle came in bearing a large vase of colorful flowers—orange, yellow and red—that really brightened up the room. They brightened up David, too.

"They're from Mom, but Margo really outdid herself, didn't she? She said to tell you hello, by the way, and hoped you'd be well soon."

"That was nice of her, and nice of you to pick them up. I know she wanted all the details."

"Well, of course, but that's part of her charm, isn't it? Besides, she really does care, and her flowers do brighten up a lot of peoples' lives. She tells me it brings good energy to a room and makes people happier."

"You're right about that. Well, now that you both are here, there's something I've wanted to tell you, something that happened in the ambulance on the way to the hospital. I think maybe I died for just a little bit in there."

The girls looked at each other, inwardly bracing themselves. *What now?*

Kyle said, "The doctor told us you nearly died. He said your heart stopped, but they took care of it after you got here, and you're okay."

"That's right. But I'm talking about something else, not just my heart stopping. I had an experience I don't really know how to talk about yet, but I wanted to try, anyway. While I was dead, or unconscious, or whatever I was, I felt like I was somewhere else. It almost seemed like a dream, but I knew it wasn't. It felt like it was really happening."

"Go ahead, Dad. Tell us."

"I do remember having trouble breathing, but then my heart stopped—the medical people told me that. What happened next was a feeling of being pulled into a tunnel, like those tunnels in the mountains, except I wasn't in a car; and then there was a light I was definitely heading for. It wasn't sunshine; it was a different kind of light. When I got far enough along, there were people waiting for me—people who have been dead for a while."

Dead people? Was he crazy as a result of this accident?

Reading their minds, David said gently, "No, I'm not crazy. I know this is hard to understand. It's hard for me to understand, too, and to find words to express just what it was like. One of the people there was my grandfather, and beside him was a figure totally made of light. That's the best I can describe it. The air was sweet, and it was the most peaceful place I have ever been. Even more peaceful than the summer place at Old Forge," he laughed.

"What did it look like, Dad? Were there buildings you recognized, like in another town?" Elizabeth was fascinated. Kyle was nervous but intrigued.

"It was nothing like that. It was almost like floating, though we seemed to be standing around while we greeted each other and talked. There was nothing scary about it. They seemed to know all about me and what had just happened. I felt so good there that I told them I loved this place and wanted to stay. Then the figure of pure light said that I had a choice to stay or to come back; and when I thought about you two and your mother, of course I said I would come back. Next thing I knew, the EMT people were bending over me to lift me onto the gurney."

"Does Mom know about this?"

"Not yet, we didn't have time to talk about it when she was here. Anyway I was still pretty groggy. No, you're the first ones I've told."

"This is an amazing story. Can we tell Esther and Arthur?"

"Of course you can. It'll be interesting to know what they think about this."

"You know what, Dad? If it's OK, I'm going to write this down for you so we remember all the details."

"Thank you for believing me, girls. It means a lot!"

Interlude, Reality Sets in

Being with Luca was like playing all the time. He was so enthusiastic about his work, about being a photographer, about New York, about life itself. How could I not fall in love with him? Except, looking back, it wasn't like falling in love. With all its pitfalls and challenges, my relationship with David was the real thing. With Luca it was like falling in love with someone you glimpse in a grocery store until you get to your car. But maybe I am being too dismissive, or not quite honest.

We have different kinds of relationships with all kinds of people, and there are different kinds of love, too. Each person can bring out a different side of ourselves; we all can manifest different personalities when we are in different circumstances, or in other stages of our lives. Who's to stay that isn't real?

Luca's enthusiasm was contagious, and he certainly was easy on the eyes, too, with that dark and slightly exotic look he had. But it was more than that. Something drew the two of us together, and I don't think either of us knew quite what that was, and we were both a little afraid of it. Perhaps something that could never be, perhaps something in another lifetime together, I still don't know quite how to explain it; but for those of you (and you are many) who have experienced it, it needs no explanation.

But when David had his accident, it jolted me back into reality. I was married, I had a husband, I had children, and that meant commitment and responsibilities. This didn't diminish the connection I felt with Luca, and I honored that. Those uncertainties and "what if's" had some purpose, murky though it was at the time. But I also knew I was needed at home. And that was honoring the deepest part of myself, not just out of duty, but also from deep love. I have never regretted that.

Chapter 14

Tori was the first to leave. Luca started to get up to embrace her, but she quickly put her hand on his. "Please, don't get up." As she started to walk away, she turned back, her face guarded against the complex emotions swirling between them. "Be safe." She walked away without looking back.

Luca fought back his desire to run after her and declare his love for her once and for all. But what was the point? She was married, and they were never going to be any more than they were now. Grabbing his wine glass, he nodded to the waiter and started toward the water. The sea never failed him as a source of comfort. He remembered playing in the water under the watchful eye of his grandfather, walking along the shore deep in discussions with friends, or courting a girl. The sea and its predictable tides settled him when his life was beset by storms. Tori would forgive him for not flying home with her, and he would see her in a month in New York. By then her feelings of betrayal would have subsided.

The hotel lobby was full of people milling around, some greeting each other, others saying goodbye. Tori wasn't ready yet to join the crowd, especially her crew, so she took the back stairs and went to her room without being seen. Her bags were already packed and waiting for the bellboy to take them down for her, and she did one more sweep to make sure nothing had been left behind. She walked to the mirror and checked her makeup. Tears were gathering just behind her eyelids, but she managed to let them stay there. She took a deep breath. *I can do this.* The telephone call she had tried to make to the girls had not succeeded, and there was nothing left to do. She picked up the phone and told the hotel desk she was ready.

Mindy rushed toward her when she saw her coming down the stairs. "We're running a bit late. The shuttle is waiting for us outside, and we've got to jump on it if we're going to make the flight to Rome." Looking around she asked, "Where's Luca? I haven't seen him. Wasn't he with you?"

"He's not coming. Is everyone else here?"

"What do you mean he's not coming? Is everything okay?"

"We'll talk about it later, Mindy. Let's just go."

There was steeliness in Tori's voice, and Mindy knew better than to ask more questions. Counting heads like a pre-school teacher, she made sure everyone was on board and ready for the short van ride to the airport. "Goodbye, goodbye Malta!" They all waved gaily out the window. They had enjoyed the work as well as the play but ready to return to New York. The adventure they shared would leave an indelible imagine on them all."

Goodbye Malta. Tori felt an ache at leaving the island, even more deeply now as the plane circled out over the sea before heading northwest. She looked down at the sparkles on the water that now looked dangerously like tears. The airport in Rome was congested with international travelers. Thank heavens for Mindy and her quiet competence and willingness always to take care of details. Tori smiled at her assistant. Mindy acknowledged the gesture and continued on with her tasks, happy to be so useful. Soon they were all on board, and Tori settled into her seat with a sigh, ready now for the long flight ahead.

Chapter 15

"Hi, Sean! Over here." Luca half-rose, waving him over to his table.

"Hi, buddy. I'm glad to see you. I was hoping you hadn't changed your mind. I hope you aren't mad at me for leading you astray! Has everyone left for Rome?"

"They're gone, but it's okay. What I said still stands. This is a journey I have to take for myself, and I'm happy we'll do it together. Did you bring the maps?"

"Let's get some food first, if that's okay. I'm starving."

After their meal they asked for coffee while they spread their maps out on the table. The papers seemed a hodge-podge of squiggles and curves, with only the Mekong River recognizable to Luca.

"Does any of this make sense to you?"

Sean nodded. As a photojournalist and activist he had been following this war in Vietnam for a few years, and the geography and names of communities rolled off his tongue as easily as did those of his own country. He bent over one of the maps and pointed out an area in the south. "This is where I would like to go. There's been a lot of fighting there, and also some stories of atrocities filtering back through the grapevine that I'd like to follow up. If the stories are true, and I have reason to believe they are, they need to be out there in the media. The lies and half-truths have to stop. We might be able to help make that happen."

Luca saw his intensity and admired him for it. Sean was a man of principle; and when he thought injustice was being done, he would fight to rectify that to the bitter end.

"Well, you'll have to bring me up to speed on these details. No telling what we're getting ourselves into, but I'm game."

They finished their coffee and folded the maps. Without saying a word, they headed to the water's edge. Gazing out over the expanse of sea, Luca focused on the shimmer of the moon, now just past full, as it played with the waves that floated to shore. A deep peace settled around him, a talisman to carry for protection from whatever came next. In spite of his protestations, he knew that Malta still lived in his heart, and it always would.

Sean left to finish packing, and Luca soon followed. He crossed the street and noticed a car idling in front of the hotel, but he dismissed it as he nodded to the doorman and started to enter the hotel. Two men stepped out of the shadows and gently yet firmly maneuvered him into the car. "Come, Luca, your father wants to see you." There was some fear, shame, and embarrassment during the ride to his family's estate. He regretted not letting them know he was here. Of course, his father's men would have spotted him. How could he have been so stupid as to think he could enter surreptitiously? His family had power and prestige, and their influence on the island was widespread. Luca had been raised a Sufi, but in the years since he had left Malta for a career in New York, they had started a Muslim Center. It had grown to be quite influential, not only on Malta but throughout Europe and the Middle East.

The car drew up to a compound, gates opening electronically to allow their entry. Luca made note of the armed guards and reaffirmed his decision to stay uninvolved. His father was waiting as he exited the car. They kissed each other in customary fashion, and then his father grabbed firmly on his forearms and held him at arm's length.

"Look at you, Luca….a grown man. You look well. We knew you were on the island and were expecting you to call. You're still in town, even though you were supposed to leave this afternoon? Who was that man you were talking to?"

"Yes, I'm still in town, but I'm leaving tomorrow with my friend Sean. You know him. We're going to Vietnam."

His father was jolted. He hadn't known that, and over coffee the questions began. There were the usual persuasions and protests. He did not want to stay in Malta and joined the family in their work at the Islamic Center. Perhaps they were doing good work, but it just wasn't for him. His life was elsewhere, and if it meant disappointing his family, then so be it.

"Luca, would you just promise me one thing? Your grandfather would like to talk with you about a project he is considering. Will you do that for him?"

His relationship with his grandfather had always been a close one. There were many happy memories from childhood of times spent with him; and the respect for the man's heart, intelligence, and talent was a part of who he was. How could he say no?

"Okay, father, but you have to understand that this trip I am taking with Sean is very important, and then I have to be back in New York in a month. I have work obligations that I just can't walk away from. You understand that, I'm sure. But tell Grandfather I'll stop here on my way back to New York and we'll talk. That's all I can promise right now."

Luca started to walk away but turned back. "Father, could you do me a favor? I was wondering where to store some of my photographic equipment while I am away, since I'm only taking one camera with me. Would it be all right if I left it here with you?"

"Of course, Luca; as you know, there is plenty of room."

It was very late when Luca was returned to the hotel. He was weary in body and soul, but his spirit was firm. This trip with Sean felt like a mission, and he was ready to begin it.

Chapter 16

It was dark when the airplane took off, and Tori was glad for the hushed atmosphere. Dinner had been served soon after the plane reached its cruising altitude, but she wasn't very hungry, mostly picking at the antipasto and bread. She had asked for a glass of wine and still held on to it when the stewardess took away the dishes. Hoping to see some stars, she looked out the window; but it had grown overcast, and the sky was dark.

"Just like I feel," she muttered to herself.

Mindy was sitting next to her and asked, "What?"

"Nothing, nothing," and they sat in silence as the aircraft hummed through the night. It should have been peaceful, but Tori couldn't relax. Her mind kept churning with the turn of events: Luca going to Vietnam, not coming back to New York for a month; shock at his impulsiveness, which was new to her. And at the forefront, her acknowledged feelings for him she had never dared admit to before.

This last was most disturbing to her. Perhaps she and David had their difficulties, and maybe she had not always been the best wife to him, working now with little time left over for the things they used to do. In the end, though, they had always been loyal and truthful to each other, and now she felt guilty at having these thoughts.

She shifted in her seat as her thoughts turned to her studio. Work was always her panacea. Her next show was going to be in three months, a small one for slect clientele to introduce some new pieces. She looked over at Mindy who was sound asleep. She adjusted her blanket and picked up one for herself from where it had fallen.

It seemed as if ages had passed since they left New York, but it had been less than a week. The time in Malta seemed like being in another world; and the peace she had experienced there would soon be shattered by the clang, clatter, and congestion of the city. She finally slept and woke just as the plane was landing.

Tori dropped her bags in the hotel room, took a quick shower, and got ready to go to the studio. She called Anna Mae to tell her she was on the way. Her amazingly competent seamstress, with her shock of premature gray hair, was already hard at work. This woman's energy knew no bounds, and it inspired Tori as the day went by in something of a blur. There were designs still unfinished, sketches to make, sessions with Anna Mae about details on the new dresses, and decisions about accessories. Without the push of staging a show, the studio was relatively quiet, with only the steady whir of a sewing machine, the rattling of sketch paper, and the occasional ringing of a telephone to intrude. Tori didn't' stop for lunch. She worked straight through, eager to get her tasks out of the way and get back to the hotel to call her family.

The silence in the hotel room, often welcomed, was now oddly oppressive, like something she could touch. Suddenly aware of how really tired she felt, she kicked off her shoes and sat down on the couch. *The girls, I've got to call them right now!* She dialed the home number first; and when there was no answer, she tried the hospital.

"Hi, Mom. When did you get back?"

"Early, early this morning, before you got up, I'm sure. I worked all day, and this is the first real chance I've had to call. How are you? How is Dad?"

"I'm good and Dad is doing much better. The doctor thinks he will be able to go home next week, but he'll have to be in bed in traction for a while."

"Great! And how is Kyle? Is she okay, too?"

"We're all fine, Mom. We're just glad you're here now. When are you coming home?"

"I have just a couple of things to finish in the morning, and then I'll be on my way. I promise. Give Kyle a hug for me and take one for yourself. And tell your father I called. I'm glad he's better."

Tori changed into a robe and slippers and got out a book she knew would put her to sleep. She climbed into bed, feeling the effects of jet lag and a long work day. But she couldn't sleep. The book was something light, a romance with an uncomplicated plot, easy to predict. *Nothing in my life is this predictable. No one really lives like the people in these books.*

Out of nowhere an image of Luca in the restaurant rose unbidden. She forced herself to stop thinking about him. Worrying about Luca would serve no one, and she knew she had to focus on David and the girls. She was relieved that David was doing better. What a scary thing! She confessed she had been too preoccupied with the burglary and Malta to really take in the full extent of his accident. As she recalled what Esther and the girls had told her, the possible outcomes collected like bad dreams.

She tossed and turned, alternately shutting her eyes only to have them pop open again. With a start that made her sit up in bed, Elizabeth's words came back in a flash. "Mom, he could have died." In that moment she realized what she had done to her family, exactly what had happened to her as a child. She had dismissed them for her own concerns.

The tears began and soon became a flood. How long had she not been there for them? Something began to break in her heart, guilt and sadness pooling into a tangle of emotions. *I'm going home tomorrow. I have to be with my family.* That resolve helped to settle her. Weariness finally won out, and she slept.

Chapter 17

DAVID had had a good night's sleep, his first since the accident, the pain now being managed well enough that it didn't wake him on and off throughout the night. The doctor was very pleased with his progress, and told him so. He also reminded David more than once how lucky he was to be alive. David could only agree. With the memory of his experience in the ambulance still fresh in his memory, he knew more than anyone how close to death he had come. How would he explain the importance of this to Tori, especially since he had a strong feeling that he had come back for reasons besides his family? He felt for the first time that some work besides supporting his family was first priority and fueling his determination to get better. He was still tired, in spite of his progress, and his energy waned more readily than he would have liked. He slipped off to sleep again hoping to be able to talk to Tori soon about his experience. He wondered what she would make of his story, and he hoped that perhaps this visit she would have time to sit and really listen to him.

He had tried to talk about it with the Rabbi when he visited earlier in the week, but the drugs made it impossible. His groggy state made it hard to clearly explain the incident without sounding like a drunk recounting a tall tale. This had been real, more real than anything thus far in his life, and David did not want to be discounted as a drug-induced person.

As David dozed, Tori drove the familiar country roads toward him, sipping a double-espresso. She had ordered it mainly because it reminded her of Malta, but also because she couldn't seem to shake off the bone-tired feeling that had been such a nuisance for her the last few years. The tiredness was all-pervasive and at times forced her to question the sanity in reestablishing her career in New York with its long commutes and even longer work hours. Preparing for this last show, plus traveling to Malta had exacerbated the issue, and she made a mental note to take a few days off, visit with the girls and David, and maybe possibly plan a vacation for herself and David at his parents' summer home on the lake. As she came around the last curve before the hospital, Tori exhaled deeply and gripped the steering wheel with determination to find the energy from deep inside to see her through the next few days. She could sleep later; her family needed her. Tori strode down the hospital corridors with determination. Had it been only a week since she ran out after Mindy's call, in a hurry to secure the jewelry she needed for the photo shoot? Guilt washed over her. *How could I have left the girls like that? And David, too*? Her heart ached, and tears were near the surface, but she kept her emotions in check. *I've got to stay strong now, for the girls, for David.* She opened the door to his room and smiled to see the girls asleep in chairs and David sleeping peacefully. She could see that his leg was still in traction, and he had some bandages on his arm where there had been some scrapes; but the machines and IVs had been removed. A rush of affection for them all surprised her with its intensity. Tiptoeing past the girls, she bent to kiss her husband. *David, my dear, dear David. We're going to be okay, aren't we?*

"How was Malta, Mom?"

She looked animated when she talked about the experience, and they could hear a subtle change in her voice and in the expression on her face when she told of meeting the woman in the café and visiting the Hypogeum. She had a softness and fragility toward them all that she infrequently showed, and the room was filled with warmth and love. David, who had wakened mid-story, felt encouraged to share his own unusual experience. The girls sat upright and Tori remained quiet as he finished. Something played at the back of her mind when he talked about mysterious figures and the light, but it slipped away before she could capture it.

"So, what do you think?" he prodded.

"I don't know what to say, David," she answered slowly. "I've never heard of anything like that before, but it sounds kind of 'far out' as the kids say. Maybe it was just the drugs to keep your heart going. Whatever the cause, it seems to have made quite an impression on you. I have to say I'm pretty intrigued, too."

"Tori, I'm glad you're here. The girls did a splendid job, bless them, but it's so good to have you back."

Tori was caught off guard. David seldom expressed himself this way, and she was touched. "Thank you, David," and she bent down to give him a quick kiss.

"Well, I hear you may be coming home before long. I'll get things set up for you, maybe in the dining room so you don't have to do the stairs." *Oh dear God, how can I do this? I can barely put one foot in front of the other these days, and now I have to nurse an injured man back to health. And go between here and New York, too. I'll have to have some help. Give me strength, Lord, give me strength.*

Chapter 18

Elizabeth and Kyle popped in to say they were going to the house with Mom and then back to school. They kissed their Dad goodbye and said they'd see him in a week. When they drove up to the house, it was hard for Tori not to feel nervous. Her last time there was rather traumatic. Tori could tell from the looks on her daughters' faces that they were thinking of that, too.

"How has it been sleeping here?" Tori quizzed them.

Kyle looked a bit sheepish. "It felt a little creepy to be at the house alone after the burglary, so we stayed with Esther and Arthur."

"Of course it would be. Good thinking. I'm glad you were safe."

She looked at them and said, "Okay, no use in putting it off any longer. We'll go in together."

They got out of the car and entered the house, but something was obviously amiss. There were tools lying near the front door, and a drop cloth covered the hallway floor. Following it to the kitchen, they found the room completely dismantled. Instantly it registered with Tori. She and David had decided some time ago to remodel the kitchen, and apparently the work had already started! Now it all came back to her! After they had gone over the plans with their architect, then they had hired the contractors and set a date for demolition. The foreman had a key, and clearly with all the upheaval of the last week this had totally escaped her mind. Devastated though she was, she wanted to put on a good face for the girls. She was just going to have to live with it. The reality was that she felt completely overwhelmed. *Oh God, what else, what else? How much more can I cope with right now? Remodels always take twice as much time and cost twice as much than you think, and I don't know how I'm going to handle this. God give me strength.* With David's coming home and needing help, and her need for some rest and relaxation, it felt like a mountain she had to climb—a very big mountain.

Elizabeth and Kyle looked uneasily at each other. "Should we not go back to school, Mom? Do you want us to stay and help out?"

"Thank you, girls, but no! You don't know how much I appreciate all you've done this week. I should have been here to help, but at least now I am here and I will handle it."

"..but what about your work in New York? Don't you have to go back soon?"

"Not right away."

They were a bit bewildered. Though they never doubted her love for them, her workaholic ways of late had made them wonder if the family played second fiddle to her career. Something must have happened while she was gone. They shrugged it off, and with waves and air kisses they headed back to school.

I miss Luca. The thought came from out of the blue, and she realized it was true. She missed his steady support, his humor, his professional camaraderie. *What is going on? I'm here with David, and I do love him, in spite of what it looks and feels like sometimes. We really do carry a deep affection for each other, and we're good parents to our girls. I just wish I knew what these feeling for Luca are all about. It's so complicated. I'll go see Esther. We haven't had a chance for a good visit in ages.*

Esther was happy to hear from Tori and eager to hear how the week had gone. "Why don't you come out and put your feet up a bit? A little country air will do you good, and you can tell me about your trip." Relieved to get out of the dust, Tori accepted. Esther had made her famous oatmeal cookies, and the scent of them led Tori into the house and back to the kitchen. The two women hugged, and Esther took off her apron. "…lemonade or tea?"

"Tea, thanks. Can we sit outside?"

They took their glasses of iced tea and a plate of cookies to the covered porch and settled into the comfortable chairs. This place had been a sanctuary for Tori and the scene of more heart-to-hearts than she could remember.

"Did you know that David is coming home this week?"

"I knew there was a possibility. That's wonderful. The doctor has been very happy with his progress, and since he's doing so well, there really is no need for him to stay in the hospital much longer."

"Oh, Esther, when I got to the house today, it looked like a disaster area. I forgot they were going to start the remodel last Friday, and of course it's too late now to delay it. Not an ideal time for David to be coming home from the hospital!"

"I'll come over in the morning and I'll help you organize; but let's not worry about all that right now. Tell me how you really are."

"I feel so guilty, Esther. I never should have left David and the girls. What is the matter with me? Am I a terrible person? Luca and Mindy could have handled things if push came to shove. How incredibly selfish I was! I was too focused on getting that layout in *Vogue*, and what that would mean to my business, and then the robbery. Even worse, and this I really hate to confess, I have *feelings* for Luca that I can't sort out yet. Forgive me, I know you love David, and I do, too. I don't know what Luca really is to me, but it feels more than professional. Now he's gone off to Vietnam, and I'm worried sick about it and can't tell anybody—except you."

"...Oh my! How can I help you, Tori?"

Tori looked out over the green fields, at the horses peacefully grazing, at the dogs sleeping under the tree. She wished her life was as peaceful as this scene. Would it ever be? Esther noticed a certain vulnerability around her friend's eyes and her mouth that made her wonder what had happened in Malta to change her. She didn't pry. She knew she would know soon enough.

"You can't imagine how much I love coming home to this. I think you heal everyone and everything you touch, dear friend," Tori sighed. "Now I must go and visit David."

"I'll be over in the morning, then—but not too early. You might want to sleep in." Esther touched her hand, "I'm really glad you're home."

"Thanks, Esther...me, too." And with that she was down the road again.

David had had a good day, with lots of rest and not much pain. He urged her to go on home when he saw her nodding off in the chair. "Sorry about the construction. I guess we both forgot, but we'll manage. See you tomorrow sometime?"

"Yes. Let them take good care of you now. And sleep well."

Tori felt a bit strange driving up to the house alone. No one would be there tonight, not David, not the girls; but it was okay. It had been a long journey, so why did she feel it was only beginning?

Chapter 19

It was several days later that David was released from the hospital. By then the house was in a state of controlled chaos, thanks mostly to Esther and all of her help. Amid the dust and debris, Tori had set up camp in the living room with a toaster, coffee pot, electric fry pan, and hot plate. They used paper plates and cups, and the powder room served as an all-purpose sink. A hospital bed accommodated the traction his broken leg still required, and a table beside his bed held some reading materials, water, and his meals. A nurse was scheduled to come by once a day to check on David's medical needs; and Louise, their long-time housekeeper, came in to clean every week.

Tori realized that her resolution to get some rest and relaxation for herself had morphed into nearly two and a half weeks of taking care of an injured husband. Frequent calls to the office kept her in touch with the work there, and Mindy and Anna Mae were doing fine. Luca was often on her mind. She couldn't help but wonder where he was, what he and Sean were doing, the kinds of situations they were finding themselves in. It all sounded very dangerous to her, and she didn't let herself dwell on it too long. Besides, it would not be long before he returned. He had promised her it would be in one month.

In some ways her life felt akin to the remodeling going on in her kitchen: tearing out the old, putting in the new. She didn't quite know what she was tearing out, or what she intended to put in; but something was beginning to stir in her. Remembering that evening in the chamber with Gabriella and the other women and how connected she had felt—not just to them but to something more ancient—brought a yearning for more experiences like that. A door had been opened that she didn't want to be closed. Who knew what might come walking in?

One afternoon David had a visitor. Tori knew she would always remember that moment—Sol coming in with a book in his right hand, his left hand holding his back, saying hello and handing the book to David. "This hasn't done a thing for me, but maybe it will help you."

The title, *Yoga, Youth and Reincarnation* by Jess Stern, made Tori think of an Indian swami sitting on a bed of nails, but she didn't give the book another thought. A few days later she saw David reading it, which shocked her. He only read the *New York Times, Time Magazine,* and his insurance periodicals for his business.

"How's the book?"

"Not bad."

Practically the highest of praise from him! When he finished it, he told her it was worth a read. That same afternoon she found a quiet corner in the living room, oblivious to the scraping and pounding coming from the kitchen, and opened the book. Four pages in, Tori was hooked. Whenever she had a spare minute, the book was in her hand.

As she described it to her friends, bells and whistles went off in her head, and she knew this was what she had been looking for and hadn't even known it. Was it true that you could be a woman and study ancient spiritual teachings? That had not been her experience in her Orthodox Jewish heritage, and the very idea was life altering. She felt exhilarated!

Mindy called from New York, breaking into these new thoughts that were swirling through her mind. "Hi, how are things with you?"

"Oh, hi Mindy, it's been a zoo here, workmen in and out, people coming to see David, trying to make meals with not much equipment. But we're surviving. David's mother has been fantastic bringing in food: brisket, chicken matzo ball soup, her famous macaroni and cheese, all made with such love."

"How's David?"

"He's doing really well. He's still in traction, but maybe for only another week. He's well enough…mainly impatient. He was much better-behaved in the hospital, probably because he was really sick and he knew no one would take orders from him. I'm taking his grouchiness to mean he wants to get out of that contraption, so I suppose that's a good thing."

"So, what's happening in New York?"

Mindy assured her they were holding down the fort but wondered if she could come down to the city for a couple of days. Tori hesitated. Hadn't she decided she needed to figure out her priorities? Waiting on David, running the necessary errands, and supervising the remodel were her priorities at the moment, but they were taxing her reserves. Perhaps a quick drive to the city would do her good. Another thing that she knew would do her good was the exercise she had just read about in the book. Finding the page she wanted, she reread the section and proceeded: moving her head downward slowly, then rolling to the right, then falling back, rolling to the left, to the chest, and then back up, three times. She repeated it, only reversing the directions. She took a deep breath and felt better. *There is something to this. I can feel it already. Wow. I can't wait to find a teacher.*

Driving the familiar road back to the city was something she could almost do blindfolded, so it was unsettling to look at the red barns and undulating curves and not quite recognize them. *What's going on? I haven't been away all that long!* She gripped the wheel and shifted in the seat uncomfortably. She told herself she would be in the city before she knew it, and that everything would be okay. She felt frightened inside, though, and repeated her pledge to herself to find a yoga teacher and learn how to relax. This stress was killing her!

Mindy and Anna Mae had already been at work for a couple of hours by the time Tori arrived. Anna Mae had the sketch for the jacket in front of her; and on Mindy's desk was a pile of correspondence, bills, requests, and phone calls that needed Tori's approval and signature.

"Hi, ladies, hope I'm not too late; the trip took a little longer than I remembered. I must have been lost for a few miles. Maybe I took a detour while my mind was on something else." She didn't tell them how odd she had felt, almost like she had been driving in an altered state.

It felt good to pick up a sketch again, to feel the silky fabric in her hand, to look around and see outfits in various stages of completion. It was what she loved to do, what she knew; and the comfort of that helped to offset the emotional turmoil and physical exhaustion she had found herself embroiled in for—how long now? She walked around, matching fabrics and designs, choosing some accessories and getting ideas for others. It was like coming home to a safe place for her, except it wasn't quite like it used to be. Something was just out of kilter, something missing.

After several hours of concerted work, Tori decided it was enough and invited the women to dinner. They chose their favorite Italian restaurant nearby, and before long they were being escorted to their usual table by the owner. Glasses of wine in hand, they talked business as they enjoyed the wonderful aromas coming from the small kitchen. Then, over coffee and dessert the talk turned more personal.

"Tori, have you heard anything from Luca? He's due back pretty soon now, isn't he?"

"Yes, less than a week—that's what he promised. And no, I haven't heard anything. I imagine he and Sean are on the move a lot, so we probably won't know anything about the trip until he shows up. I'm trying not to worry about the film. He promised to send the photographs to me, but maybe I misunderstood. Perhaps he'll return with the film and photographs in hand."

Mindy could tell Tori was getting more and more agitated thinking about Luca and the film and decided to quickly pursue a different line of conversation.

"How are David and the girls?"

"Fine….fine….Did I tell you two about that book I'm reading? I've never read anything like it. It's about yoga and a lot of other stuff, and quite frankly it's blowing my mind. I'll buy copies for you if you would like. I wish I weren't so exhausted. I'd love to tell you more about it."

Tori decided to stay the night in the city, considering the incident driving in earlier. Getting ready for bed, she felt dizzy; then she began to tremble and had a hard time buttoning her nightgown. *I'm just tired. I'll be okay in the morning.*

Interlude, Yoga Book

The discovery of the book, Youth, Yoga, and Reincarnation, began my spiritual odyssey. I had no idea at the time I was about to embark on this journey, but how could I? For many years, the course of my life had been that of wife and mother, keeper of the hearth, nurturer of others. More recently, the success of the design business I had resumed in New York had been a pleasant surprise. I had missed the rewards of that life. No matter that I worked harder and harder, however, clearly something was lacking. What eluded me had no name until that book appeared. As if the words were lit, I read 'one of the requisites of yoga (is that) it leads to truth.' In my unstable early life, nothing had made sense. There was no real truth, there was no understanding—only confusion. Was this what I had been looking for—truth and peace of mind? When had I ever truly had that? Certainly not as a child, and then not in my marriage, either. The health benefits attributed to a yoga practice appealed to me, also. Perhaps it would help me be less tired, I thought, less tense. As I delved further into the book, and understood yoga as a 'union of body and mind with the supreme spirit', my imagination soared along with my heart. Somewhere deep in my psyche I knew what they were talking about. It felt like coming home.

Chapter 20

DAVID asked about her venture into the city. "The fun part was working with the new fabric we found—you know how I love that. Oh, and I took Anna Mae and Mindy to that little Italian restaurant down the street we love, you know the one, Café Gino, I think; so it wasn't all work and no play."

"Glad to hear that. You were due for a little play."

"David, you know, I've been pretty engrossed in that book, *Yoga, Youth, and Reincarnation*. I know you told me it was worth a read, but I must say I am astonished that you would read something like this. I am completely taken by it. I've been doing some of the exercises they suggest on my own, and I've decided I want to find a yoga teacher and take some classes. There's nothing like that here in town, so I'm not sure where to start. I must admit that right now I feel too tired to even think of doing those exercises; but maybe if I start, I might get more energy, just like it happened for the author of the book."

"It can't hurt. I do agree with the author that stress can be very damaging to one's health. Just make sure the teacher isn't a fanatic who insists that you become a vegetarian. I couldn't stand it if you didn't cook for me any longer. Some of the spiritual stuff they talk about is a little far out of the ballpark for me, but as exercise it really can't hurt if you do it right."

David was a lot more open to all of this than she would have expected. It shouldn't have been a surprise, though, because he had often been open to other ideas before his friends were. Besides, with his work with the country club and now this new project, David had already shown his acceptance of other religious or spiritual ideas. "Live and let live," he always said, and he practiced what he preached.

Her body was beginning to relax.

"I have to say, the trip did wear me out. Can I get you anything before I go upstairs for a little rest?"

"Thanks, I can't think of anything."

"I'll be down in a couple of hours."

Tori wearily climbed the stairs. Her legs felt like lead, and she found herself gripping the railing as she almost pulled herself up. *I'm just going to rest a couple of hours, and then I'll be fine. I'm just tired, that's all....Just so tired.*

Chapter 21

THE next level of physical therapy began for David. The time in the hospital and in bed at home for weeks had been hard for such an active man, and he was more than ready to be up and about working on his projects. His ribs were still very sore, as was his leg, and getting used to the crutches took some doing; but his determination to be independent won out.

He had been doing work from home whenever he was clear-headed enough—the painkillers initially made him a bit woozy—and the phone rang constantly with business calls. His secretary ran things efficiently at the office, but there were letters to dictate to her and clients to speak to about problems they were having. They also sometimes called just to say hello and see how he was doing. David was a popular guy.

The remodeling project gradually created less chaos. The only noise the contractors generated was with electrical and plumbing work; once they finished that, they could do the painting, and then they would be done!

Tori, on the other hand, was *not* doing as well. Her presence in New York had been required more times than she had anticipated. She didn't always stay overnight, as she didn't want to leave David alone; but the trips back and forth in one day were alarmingly tiring. She and Mindy were almost frantic about the photographs. *Vogue* had called twice wanting to see them. Tori explained that they had not yet heard from their photographer, who should have been back by now; and they had no way to get in touch with him. The models had gone on to other jobs, and it was impossible to put together another shoot on such short notice. It was almost certain that *Vogue* would have to go ahead without them. Mindy thought that Tori should come to the city and talk with the editors at the magazine to try to salvage the layout.

Tori avoided turning on the television these days. The news was always bad: scenes of battles, prisoners of war, executions, napalm dropping on innocent citizens, children getting burned, politicians pontificating, and people marching in the streets. It made her wonder what this world was coming to. Underlying her angst was the knowledge that Luca and Sean were somewhere in the middle of all that. *Well, they have each other to get through this,* and she sent up a little prayer for their safety.

Her mind was in a constant spin with worry about Luca, her contract with *Vogue*, where the photos were, whether the remodel would be done soon so their life could get back to normal, and whether David would heal totally from his injuries. She worried about herself, too. She was having more trouble concentrating, her sleep was fitful most nights, and her appetite was poor. She knew she should go to a doctor. She wondered what was wrong, but she just didn't have the time to do anything about it right then. She also had promised herself to start yoga classes. She thought it could help her, but she didn't even have the time or energy to pursue that. The first thing she had to do was to get to New York and see if there was any way to stall for some time with *Vogue* and work with Mindy on locating Luca.

When she reached her office, Mindy and Anna Mae were waiting for her. "Sit down, Tori. I have some bad news." Her thoughts immediately turned to Luca. *Oh, god, no. Don't let anything happen to him. Make him be all right.*

"*Vogue* just called while you were on your way, and they've shelved the project. They said they just couldn't wait any longer and had to go ahead with something else. Maybe later they could take a look at the photos, they said, but for now it was a no go."

It was all Tori could do not to cry. They had all worked so hard. The layout would have been so good. The boost to her image in the fashion community was no small potatoes, either; plus, that would mean more work and more money. She looked at Mindy and Anna Mae.

"I, I don't know what to say." Usually Tori could pull herself together in a hurry when she had to, but this was too much. All that work for naught? What did it mean for the business, for these two loyal employees?

"I am so sorry. I am so sorry."

Quietly she asked, "Can you two take some time off while I figure out what to do? Will you be okay?"

She looked around at the sunny studio, a little oasis in the middle of the city where she had been living out her dream. She had always wanted to create designs for women to make them look beautiful and to feel good about themselves. She couldn't help but feel that perhaps she had created a little happiness along with her fashions, and that thought helped soothe her ragged emotions. She wasn't sure just what they would do next, but she would take some time to sort it out.

"Well, I'm going to see what I can work on at home. I've had a few ideas this past week, but I've had no time to go farther. Maybe I can doodle around with them while things get straightened out." She started for her office but turned back. Looking at Mindy and Anna Mae with affection, she said to them, "Thank you, for everything."

When she was out of earshot, Mindy and Anna Mae looked at each other. "Do you notice anything different about Tori? I can't remember when I've seen her look so completely fatigued."

It wasn't until Tori got in her car that the full reality of the situation hit her. It felt like her head was going to explode as the unanswered questions presented themselves one after another. Where was Luca? Why hadn't he at least sent those photos? How embarrassing to have lost *Vogue*. Would she ever get another chance? Why did David have to get on that stupid horse in the first place? Why did they forget about the remodel that couldn't have come at a worse time? Why was she always so tired, so sleepless, and not hungry?

Ignoring the beautiful countryside, she drove straight to the drugstore in town to pick up David's prescription. At least she had remembered that—no small feat with everything imploding around her. As she got out of the car, she had to grab onto the door. There it was again, the dizziness, that strange feeling that everything was unreal and that she might fall over any minute. With effort she straightened up and and made her way to the pharmacy, vowing to go straight home and lie down for a little while. "Hi Bill, I'm here to pick up David's prescription. Is it ready?" And that was the last thing she remembered as the world went black.

Chapter 22

THE EMTs were there in less than five minutes to whisk Tori to St. Elizabeth's. In the emergency room they soon roused her, but her voice was very weak. She seemed lost and could not tell them her name, date, or the president of the United States—standard questions to rule out brain injury.

"Where am I?" She caught the lapel of the ER doctor as he bent over to look at her pupils.

"You fainted in the pharmacy. Do you remember? You are safe now, in the hospital. Have you taken any drugs? Did you hit your head when you fell?"

Seeing that she had lapsed back into unconsciousness, the doctor ordered a full work up of her blood and started her on an IV. The woman was clearly dehydrated with an arrhythmic heart rate, but it seemed in all likelihood that this was the result of some long-standing physical and mental issues.

"Get a room ready for her on the third floor, and we'll take her up as soon as I get the lab results. Her family will be here any minute."

Arthur picked up David the minute he got his call.

"This looks unfortunately familiar. Didn't we just do all this?"

"Sure seems like it, Arthur. Thanks for coming in for the replay. I hope Tori is okay. She really hasn't been herself for a while. I think she's just pushing too hard. I hope that's all it is."

When they came into the hospital, David introduced himself and a nurse directed them to Tori's room. The doctor met them there, surprised to recognize David, now on crutches.

"Mr. Litchfield, your wife seems to be suffering primarily from exhaustion. Has she been depressed recently? Under a lot of stress? I think it would be wise to keep her here for a few days, just to see how things go. Is that all right?"

"...of course. You might be right on all accounts. I have been recuperating myself, so she has not been sharing with me all of her problems; but I can imagine they have been burdening her."

The doctor left and David turned his attention to Tori. She looked so pale lying on the white sheets, her beautiful eyes closed. "Is she conscious?" he asked the nurse nearby.

"Yes. She's just asleep. The doctor ordered some medication to help her rest. Why don't you come back tomorrow, maybe around noon? She should be more alert then."

David leaned over to kiss her, whispering in her ear, "I'm leaving for a while, Tori, but I'll be back tomorrow. Rest well, sweetheart. I love you."

Contrary to her peaceful countenance, Tori was *not* well. Something had shut off within her. She had depleted all her reserves, and for self-preservation her body had refused to continue in the same manner. Weakened by dehydration, lack of rest, worry and disappointment, her system was overwhelmed. No one looking on could see the storms, the dreams, the visions that coursed through her mind. No one could see the energy that was being released, the remembrances of old worlds and the opening to the new, the stream of consciousness that flowed. Her nerves and brain were at war within her, and on some level she completely surrendered to it. It seemed okay to her that she never wake up. Maybe she was already dead? How could one tell, anyway?

The first thing she saw were clouds. She was a child looking up at the sky, and then the clouds took form and became creatures that looked like her idea of angels. They swooped low and she could feel their beneficence. Immersed in their loving kindness, she was not frightened when other, stranger figures arrived. Some looked like Egyptian royalty, but they were very tall, much taller than any person on earth at this time. Inside their dwellings she saw interesting designs on their walls, geometric in shape but different from the patterns she was used to seeing in her work. They seemed to mean something to the people there, but she couldn't grasp quite what it was. In the mixture of beings that swirled all around her was a Cro-Magnon man who stopped what he was doing and looked in her direction before he proceeded on his path. Native Americans and other indigenous people joined the throng, along with a young man who seemed to be spending a lot of time with them, perhaps learning their customs. Goddesses, yogi, relatives who had passed over with whom she could converse, someone teaching her how to breathe in a different way, all went by in a seemingly endless parade. Past and future melded together into an eternal now that had no beginning and no end. She was watching it as well as being a part of it. Nothing was really separate; it was all part of a whole. For the first time in her life she felt that she was 'one' with the universe.

Interlude, Breakdown

My breakdown was inevitable; I'm sure you could see it coming. I had never learned to take care of myself, to value my own health and well-being on any level. When I was a child, I was a second mother to my baby brother. As an adult, all of my energy went out to my marriage, my daughters, my work. What was left was given to the rest of the family or the community. A few days before I fainted at the pharmacy, I stood in the shower and thought I was going to die. I didn't think anybody who was that tired could live.

I remember having chicken pox as an adult and spending a week in bed with two little girls for company and no one to help me. David was at work all day. And my parents, who had been there to care for the children while David and I were away for the weekend, would not stay. It was always like that, it seemed. I did manage to get through those times, but I had not yet learned who I was, or to ask for what I needed. That took time, but the breakdown was the catalyst that engendered change.

I know now that those situations in our lives have the greatest teachings for us. How else would we stop and listen? Pay attention? Hear what spirit is telling us? Something has to stop us in our tracks so we can change course. This was mine. How could I not be grateful for that lesson?

Interlude, Luca in Vietnam

Bits and pieces of days and places whirled around nonsensically in his head, and the distinction between reality and nightmare disappeared. How long had it been? Where was he? Nightmare reality or just nightmare, there was nothing left to do but surrender to it. Sweet faces of villagers crouched over him with food; long rides on trucks were followed by longer stretches through dense jungle. His body, now gaunt and scarred, felt disassociated from his mind and was savage-like in its stench and filth. What had happened? He remembered the weeks of rain and the screams and the hunger. And Sean—he remembered his sweet buddy's wink and salute before they dragged him away. He hadn't seen Sean after that, which was not a good sign.

And how had he escaped? Explosions, fire, more screaming—he couldn't remember; but the AWOLs he had met up with heading to Hue helped as much as they could with a pair of boots, a pair of pants, a compass, and some food. Their agenda was not his, and they felt he was safer alone with a much-coveted knife courtesy of the US Army. Head to Thailand, they had encouraged. Go south to Saigon. Get out of here. You speak French, you look French. Let them think you are French. They hate our guts. Don't speak English, man, whatever you do.

Choppers overhead… could it be Americans dropping food? One bundle they dropped was tangled in the canopy. Waiting undercover, watching as the group left in trucks overflowing with bundles, grabbing the bundle left behind. Not food. Whatever it was, it cut the hunger and eased the pain. Numbness, brown powder from the gods, and the rains—torrential in their fury—that soaked him while he walked through flooded fields. And always there were the friendly brown-skinned people—so kind, sweet, and compassionate.

How many months had he traveled, deliriously ravaged? Finally the rain stopped and then the broiling unbearable heat. Not alone now. Late March and people were pouring into Saigon from the central highlands, desperate to outrun the encroaching communist troops. Shots whistling around, stray rockets, families tragically separated . . . blind panic. The Communists were advancing quickly, and there was a call for an evacuation of all defense attachés and non-essential personnel among rumors of beheadings. And then the mortar attack on Tan Son Nhat airport. Choppers from aircraft carriers evacuating

Americans to Clark Air force Base in the Philippines. Luca fared no better than the local civilians clawing and bribing for safe passage. With no visa and no passport he joined thousands of refugees crowding onto fishing boats heading out into the South China Sea. His boat avoided the harrowing fate of most others, which were terrorized by scavenging pirates and typhoons. Finally some luck…a friendly vessel offering safe passage to Manila.

Chapter 23

Where am I? What am I doing here? As the room came into full focus, Tori felt an IV in her arm and saw a vase of fall flowers gracing her bedside table. *The girls, I bet, or David.* There was a card beside them, and she reached over to open it. *To my love, feel better soon, David.*

Tears came to her eyes. This was from a man who carefully guarded his feelings, especially verbally. *Bless him, he must have been really worried about me.*

A nurse appeared at her side. "Good afternoon, Mrs. Litchfield. I see you're awake! How are you feeling?"

"I'm not sure just yet. Is it afternoon? I must have slept a long time."

"Longer than that. You've been asleep for two days. You really needed the rest, my dear. You were pretty exhausted when you came in."

" I still feel pretty tired. Two days, huh? I've never slept that long. Has anyone been in?"

The nurse assured her that David, Esther, and Dorothy had all been by. *Dorothy had been here, too? I remember the girls told me that Grandma and Grandpa had come down a couple of days after David's accident. So she's here again? I hope she's still here.*

"Could I have the phone? I'd like to call David and let him know I'm awake."

"The other nurse has already called. He wanted to know the minute you opened your eyes, and I suspect he's already on his way."

David had been in consultation with the doctor as well as the psychiatrist. It seemed that Tori's collapse had been brought on by an overload of work, not taking care of her health properly, and perhaps deep disappointment over the turn of events at her design studio. David had known things were not going well with *Vogue*, but he hadn't known about the cancellation of the layout until he talked with Mindy. He could only imagine what this must have done to Tori. The news of losing that must have been devastating, and his heart ached for her.

The doctor suggested a month's rest, perhaps a residential place of some kind, even a hospital, but David knew Tori would balk at that. He had an idea; maybe the family place at the lake would appeal to her, and he called his mother to see if she could help. She and Tori were very close, and they both loved being there. When he proposed this to the doctor, he agreed as long as there was a doctor close by, and that there were no unsettling distractions. The psychiatrist requested that he have a session with Tori before she left to see if there were any issues that needed immediate attention, and to suggest medications to help alleviate any anxiety she might have in the beginning. This, of course, was contingent upon Tori's approval.

When David clumped into her room on crutches, his heart caught in his throat. She gave him her usual radiant smile, but she looked small and wan. He smiled and almost shyly said, "Hello, sweetheart."

Her 'hello' was nearly a whisper. She nodded toward the flowers. "And thank you for those. They're beautiful."

He bent to give her a kiss and straightened up. "How are you feeling today?"

"I'm not quite sure yet. Still a bit tired."

Dr. Brown strode into the room, smiling at Tori. "They let me know you were awake, so I came right over. I hope you're feeling better."

"I'm not sure yet. I hope so."

He told her what the doctors had found out and about their recommendation for a complete month of rest away from any stress or responsibility.

Tori looked at David, and he nodded in agreement. "Where could I go to get that kind of rest?"

"We talked about that. I told the doctor about the house at the lake. I know you love it there, and it would be especially quiet and peaceful this time of year. What do you think?"

"Well, that might be good. I'd have to get somebody to come in and help until I'm on my feet."

"I thought of that, too. How about my mom? I've asked her if she'd be willing to do that, and she jumped at the chance. She loves you so much, you know."

Tori began to cry in earnest. A month at her favorite place, with a favorite person, no work, no obligations—she could do that.

David sighed in relief. "I'd miss you, but I'm glad you like the idea. You know, you've always said that place held some magic."

He held up his hand as she began to utter objections. He knew what they would be. "I'm really fine, just healing; and we have Louise to clean the house and cook for me."

She couldn't help but agree. After they were gone, the psychiatrist knocked on the door and asked for permission to come in. He was a large man but a very gentle soul, and he probed delicately about how she felt about the work disappointment, and about why she was working so hard. Her answers were mostly evasive, but he could read in her responses that there was something deeper she was struggling with. He would need time with her to allow her to open up and confide in him. The paramount issue of first priority was rest. They could work on those matters later. He handed her a prescription for some sedatives to help her sleep. She at first refused medication but finally agreed to take it along, 'just in case'.

The details of getting ready were simple. Esther came over and together they packed what she would need for a few weeks. Not much, really, just pants and sweaters and some walking shoes, underthings and pajamas, a warm coat. At the last minute she put in a notebook she had picked up somewhere because she liked the velvety texture of the cover. There were books already at the cottage, and the little library in town had a fairly decent selection, too. A small supermarket, a few restaurants, they would be fine.

It was just before Halloween that Dorothy came to fetch her. Tori waved goodbye to David as he stood in the doorway, waving a crutch. *Whatever I am in for, I'm ready.* She wondered where that random thought came from, but shrugged her shoulders and relaxed as Dorothy drove them to the lake.

Chapter 24

For the first time in a long while, Tori allowed herself the luxury of being cared for. Indeed it was not even a luxury; it was a necessity. She simply could not go on with the life she had been leading and finally knew it. Her body, mind, and soul were totally depleted. *What is it going to take to get healthy again?* She was too tired even to contemplate an answer. The drive through the countryside along a road sheltered by trees was a trip back in time. Images of her first summers there, weighted with the care of two babies, frustrated with a marriage that was no longer viable, and anxious about her lack of training in basic child care and household skills left her feeling unworthy and unloved. Dorothy fixed that. Recognizing the signs of a confused and even frightened young wife and mother, she took her under her wing. *Where in the world would I be now if it had not been for this mother-in-law? Where would my girls be?* Tori, so close to tears these days, nearly broke down at the thought. Now she was back again, needing rest and healing. *I hope Dorothy's magic works again.*

Before she knew it, a glimpse of the little camp down the narrow lane and the gleam of the lake beyond it beckoned her home. That word caught her up: *home.* When had she really felt at home, in her house or in her skin? Maybe in her studio, but probably never as much as here.

The two women went about opening the house that had been closed for a month and a half, after which Dorothy went to the local market to shop for supplies. She was determined to get some meat back on those bones of Tori's and chose ingredients for meals she knew her daughter-in-law enjoyed. *No more of that crazy fasting for spiritual awakening; she's got to get strong, which means she has to eat, and I know how to do that.*

While Dorothy was out, Tori gravitated to the little sunroom where she could look out over the water. The late October sun still held warmth, and the comfort of its rays across her face brought an appreciation of simple pleasure. *I've missed this.*

At bedtime they hugged goodnight; then Dorothy held her at arm's length, looked steadily into her eyes, and said, "Tori, you will be well."

"Thank you," she whispered.

Sleep did not come as easily as she thought it might. She was tired, in spite of the rest in the hospital, but this time her mind was not filled with exotic images. Instead, she saw her little girls and her own younger self in these rooms those long summers ago. Tori's feelings with her babies had run the gamut from delight and love to fear. *How can I take care of a baby? How can I love this darling child without damaging it? Who can tell me what to do so I can do it right?* She had looked at their beautiful little faces, trying to find an answer there, but they had simply gazed back at her and smiled as she snuggled them into her arms. Feeling exhausted and trapped, she had held them close and hoped that her tears wouldn't wet their silky little heads.

Dorothy stepped into the breach that summer years ago by teaching Tori how to cook, how to care for her children, and to feel love and respect for herself.

"Tori, come. I will show you how to make this dish with potatoes and sauerkraut. It isn't hard. We will do it together."

Tori had never had that kind of experience with another woman, and she was hesitant at first, fearful of making a mistake.

"Are you sure? I haven't cooked anything before. I might not do it right. Maybe nobody will eat it."

But the older woman got out her apron, put another apron on Tori, and soon they were happily at work in the kitchen, laughing and talking as they made food for everyone. No one yelled at her. No one told her she couldn't do anything right. The babies were nearby, entranced by the activity at the table, and laughed as they joined in the fun. It was a happy time.

These memories finally lulled Tori to sleep. *This was a good place to come back to. David was right. Here I can heal.*

The days began to take on a rhythm that was predictable and soothing: lots of rest, good food, walks in the woods behind the house, quiet talks in the evening before the fire. She and Dorothy reminisced, laughed over family stories, read books they got at the library, went to bed early. It was simple, slow, and just what she needed.

One afternoon Tori announced that she felt strong enough to walk into town. Most of the leaves had gone from the trees, leaving only the evergreens to guard the lake against winter. She put on her warm sweater, tied a scarf around her neck, and started out. It felt good to venture a little farther from the house, and soon she was striding down the road at a good clip, surprising herself. In town she stopped in a café for some hot chocolate and idly perused the bulletin board while her order was being prepared.

Among notices of lost cats, rooms for rent, and spaces for boat storage was a card that read simply *Astrologer* with a name and phone number. Astrology? Tori had heard of it and sometimes read the little blurbs in the paper telling her what she might expect that day, even though few of the predictions came true. Was this the same thing, or something different? On a whim, she called the woman's number when she got home and made an appointment with Dawn for the next day.

It wasn't at all what she had expected. There was no crystal ball, no giant hooped gold earrings, no head scarves and full skirts with bangles. Instead, a young woman in a pair of beige slacks and a soft blue sweater welcomed her and directed her to a comfortable chair. She asked Tori why she had come. Tori shrugged her shoulders. "I really don't know, frankly. I saw your sign in the café down the street and decided to call you. I confess I don't know anything about astrology, but I *am* curious."

Dawn nodded. She told Tori she would work up her chart, and Tori provided the information about place and time of birth. Soon they were talking about transits and voids, terms far beyond Tori's present understanding. A few days later, Dawn showed her what she had found in her chart. The most interesting thing to Tori was that the chart showed how difficult her marriage would be. "I don't need an astrologer to tell me that!" she laughed. Still, it was interesting that it came up so strongly. "Just a minute, I think someone wants to come in with a message for you," Dawn said. She began to speak in a slower, deeper voice. "You are not required to learn again, but only to remember." And then another message came. "What you would seek to give to others, be willing to accept for yourself." Then all was quiet.

As Tori sat wide-eyed, Dawn explained that sometimes she 'channeled' other spirits, and this time St. Germaine had come through for her. "It is an honor to receive these messages," she said. "You are truly blessed."

That evening as she thought about the events of the day, Tori recalled the green notebook she had picked up at the last minute. *Now, where did I put that? I need to write this down before I forget it.* She found it and opened the cover of her first journal.

Late fall can be a melancholy time with darkness falling earlier and the earth slowing down for winter; but for Tori it was the kind of quiet she needed, both inside and out. Dawn had told her about meditation as a way to reach this kind of stillness, and Tori began a practice that she hoped to continue at home.

Finally the last day came. She and Dorothy closed up the house and drove just ahead of the first snowstorm. Tori looked back as they exited the narrow lane now filled with dried leaves. The lake was choppy and the house half-shrouded in fog. *It's time to leave, time to get back to my life, but it's going to be different. I'm better, thanks to Dorothy's wonderful care, and I feel strong enough for whatever comes next. Thank you Universe!*

Interlude, Old Forge

I think about those days at the lake as my first real beginning of friendship with women. I had girl friends at school, of course, but the relationship with Dorothy was on a different level and so comforting to me. I wonder if I could have forged such strong relationships with Esther and others if I had not had this patient woman to show me how? She not only took care of my children, she took care of me, too, in so many ways. As I grew, so did our relationship, and it was always most precious to me.

One of the reasons I married David was because I wanted a mother-in-law. This is true! I had always loved the story of Naomi and Ruth, and I wanted a relationship like that. I'm sure most of you know the story of these two women, one a mother-in-law, the other a daughter-in-law. Naomi had gone to Moab with her husband and their two sons. After her husband died, her two sons married. When the sons, too, died, Naomi decided to return to her own people and exhorted her daughters-in-law, Orpah and Ruth, to return to their own families instead of going with her. Orpah did return home, but Ruth insisted on staying with Naomi, and they returned together.

Instead of Naomi and Ruth we were Dorothy and Tori, but the feeling was the same. Like Ruth, I truly felt 'whither thou goeth, I will go; and whither thou lodgest, I will lodge; thy people shall be my people, and thy God my God.' When David's job took us out of the city, it meant that we would be living closer to his family, and that sweetened any bitterness I might have about leaving the city and my career.

Dorothy was a genuinely kind person; her eyes were warm and welcoming, and she had a huge heart. Later on she confessed that she had been a bit afraid of me at first because I was so pretty. I, in turn, told her that I was nervous about living up to any expectations about being a wife or mother because I didn't have a clue about either one. In spite of our initial trepidations, I was welcomed into the family with love, and that was that. Dorothy took the girls to her house every Friday night from the time they were tiny babies, cooked wonderful food for us, and could be counted on in any emergency. My own mother had looked at Dorothy when she first met her and announced to me, "That is your mother." It rang true. Dorothy and I had a soul connection that was sustained for our whole time together.

My life had never been easy. My mother's demands and criticisms took their toll, so when I had my own children I was unsure and frightened. It wasn't until they were four years old that I could begin to relax and care for them with more ease and therefore more joy. I was determined to make a better life for my daughters than I had ever had, and David and I did create a strong family. Still, it took time until I finally knew who I was and could act accordingly.

The girls and I and Dorothy spent every summer at Old Forge, while the men worked in town and came down on weekends. It was truly my other home; but until I was ordered to rest for a month, I had not fully appreciated what a haven it was. As I said in the beginning, the house at the lake is where my soul is most at peace; Dorothy helped plant the seeds of that peace in its fertile soil.

Interlude, Luca in Manila

Luca was tired, drenched in sweat, his heart pounding when he dragged himself into the Manila hospital. There was pressure behind his eyes, pain exploded in his stomach, and tears streamed uncontrollably as his body heaved and contorted in despair and overwhelm. Could this nightmare really be over? Would someone finally be able to help him make sense of it? For the first time in months Luca thought about Tori and New York City. It was not possible to make sense of that life. Were people really posing in diaphanous fabrics among ancient ruins as innocent children were being massacred?

Another kind brown face came close to his, asking his name. No words came out of his mouth. Was he dead.......why couldn't he talk? He tried desperately to communicate through his eyes and cooperate with the emergency personnel moving him onto a gurney and inserting IVs into his arm. Scenes—horrible scenes—whirled in his brain, and then a screeching nothingness.

Nothing, that is, until the most peaceful energy filled his awareness...was it in the room, in a dream, this pure, golden, luminous hallucination? It grew more intense, rays emanating in all directions until there was nothing but the Light and an instinctual knowing of what was happening. Warm healing love, pure and simple in its magnificence, infiltrated every pore, every cell, and every molecule of his being. The war inside and out subsided; all turmoil subsided, all anger, fear and painful memories receded...supplanted with reassurance that all was 'as it was meant to be' and that all was perfect.

Soon he began to talk, and talk he did, non-stop for twelve hours, as nurses hovered around listening to his maniacal ranting and jubilation, waiting for the crash. It would be seventy-two hours later when he awoke hungry. First he would get food, and then he would find a way to India. Sean had mentioned having gone to India to see a guru who wore dark glasses and worked with Westerners. It had changed Sean profoundly; it was why he had gone to Vietnam instead of pursuing a career in the film industry. Luca marveled at the similarities now between him and Sean. Fashion? How could he have ever thought that was his calling? He must get to India and find this guru.

Chapter 25

"Luca!" Tori sat straight up in bed as images of men in uniforms and faint sounds of gunfire invaded her sleep. Her palms were sweaty and her heart was racing. Slowly she eased out of bed and crept down the hall without waking anyone to get a drink of water and take some deep breaths to calm her panic. The dream was so real that the smallest details stood out sharply: jungle foliage, a river nearby, brown uniforms, hands tied with rope. *But whose?* Her hands shook. Luca still had not returned, nor had he sent any messages. Not knowing where he was or what was happening was the hardest part. If only she could hear from him, if only she knew he was all right!

Tori sat on the couch for a few minutes with her glass of water while her heart returned to its normal rhythm. *What was that all about?* She certainly had vivid dreams from time to time, but this was different, especially in its intensity. She decided to do a short meditation as long as she was up. Sitting on the floor in a lotus position, just as it said in the book, she held her hands on her knees with palms facing upward and began to focus only on her breath, in and out, in and out, until she was calm and relaxed again. *This stuff really works. It really does.*

After her return from her sojourn in Old Forge, it had been hard to integrate herself back into the old routine. David was happy to have her home, but he didn't fully understand that she was still somewhat fragile. Running a household again, having a social life with David's clients, and finding time to rest was a daily juggling act. As soon as she returned, Tori met with the doctor, and he was pleased with how she was recovering. To continue on that track she promised to stop smoking, limit her caffeine to one cup of coffee in the morning, eat regular meals, and take time to relax. A simple regimen, but one she had failed to follow for too long. In addition, he was adamant that she not return to the studio in New York for some months, if ever. Before her breakdown, the doctor's suggestions would have fallen on deaf ears, but the time in Old Forge had helped her to shift her priorities. The quieter life had more appeal than she ever would have imagined, and now all she wanted to do was to begin a yoga practice. But first she had to find a teacher.

Wondering where to start, she picked up the *Yoga, Youth and Reincarnation* book for inspiration. She called it her *Bible* and had opened it so often that the pages were dog-eared. This time she noticed a name written on the inside cover: Dr. Gerald Green. *So that is who this book belongs to. Hmm, I don't remember seeing that before.* Tori knew of a Dr. Green who lived near a friend of hers, and she picked up the phone. Tori told Sophie about seeing the name and wondered if she knew him.

"Sure I do," she said. "We ski together. Are you looking for a doctor?"

"No, I'm not. I'm looking for a yoga teacher, and I thought he might know of one since his name was in the book. Or do you know anything about classes being offered anywhere?"

Sophie recalled that the YWCA wanted to start a class, but they hadn't found a teacher yet. "Why don't I just give you Dr. Green's number? He's a nice guy and wouldn't mind if you gave him a call. Maybe he knows more about this."

That evening he and Tori talked. "I think I can help. I know a teacher who travels the state to teach classes wherever she's invited. Here, I'll give you her number."

Tori made the necessary calls, and yoga classes were scheduled to begin at the YWCA after the holidays.

But first there was Thanksgiving. The kitchen remodel had been completed in her absence, and she was happy with the results. Her sage green cabinets were especially pleasing to her—no one else was using that color yet. There would be a full table and lots of planning and work to do in a short time. The girls would be home from school in time to help, Mindy had said she was bringing a friend, and Esther and Arthur were coming. Dorothy and her husband Max were bringing the kosher turkey plus a kosher brisket, and Tori would organize everything else.

Mindy was the last to arrive. When asked where her friend was, she said quickly, "Oh, something came up for him. He was sorry he couldn't be here." Tori pulled her into the house and showed her where to hang her coat, then went off to deal with the last-minute details. As family and friends gathered around the beautiful table, Tori asked everyone to hold hands and say what they were grateful for this year. The answers surprised and nearly overwhelmed her. Everyone was grateful for her and David, for their recovery, for all the love and energy they gave to their family and friends, and for just being here together. In a soft voice she said, "And I am so grateful to all of you." David couldn't bring himself to speak, but his nod to each one spoke of his thanks, too. Tori wanted to include Luca in their litany of gratitude, but she couldn't bring herself to speak his name. They probably wouldn't understand, and she didn't know what to be thankful for regarding him, so she silently said a little prayer for his safety and let it sail out to the universe.

Later the men, along with Elizabeth and Kyle, retired to the den to watch the football game. From the living room the women could hear their cheering or complaining, depending on how the team was faring. They all looked at one another and Dorothy ventured, "It's quieter in here." They agreed, but of course their chatter soon generated its own volume. Tori wanted to tell them about her discovery of yoga, and her excitement over the possibility of a class in town was palpable. It was too far away for Dorothy and Mindy to come, but Esther promised to give it a try. "I wonder what the men are going to think about this yoga thing? Will they think we've lost our minds?"

"David read the book and seemed impressed. Maybe he'll give Arthur the word," said Tori.

Dorothy and Max left right after the game, and Elizabeth and Kyle were right behind them to join a gathering at a college friend's house. David and Arthur were still in the den.

"What do you say, girls—want to join me in a glass of wine or something to eat? We can take it upstairs to my little sitting room. We don't need to hear this football game rehashed over and over before something else begins."

Esther declared she couldn't eat for another week, but a glass of wine sounded good. Mindy nodded in agreement. Sharing a bowl of mixed nuts balanced on the ottoman in front of them, they kicked off their shoes and curled up on the blue velveteen couch.

Chapter 26

"Tori, how was your month in Old Forge? Was it restful? You seemed pretty tired last time I saw you."

"It was just what the doctor ordered, Mindy, thanks; but I've missed you and Anna Mae. How're you doing?"

Mindy had gulped half of her wine by then, and her hand shook as she looked for a place to put down her glass. Her eyes sought Tori's, but it was Esther who noticed that Mindy was about to break into tears. Quickly she moved closer to the young woman and took her hand. "Mindy, what's wrong? You can tell us, honey. You're among friends."

Esther and Mindy had met on a number of occasions, and they both had warm feelings for each other. Esther admired the way Mindy ran Tori's business, keeping things organized and running smoothly for her boss. She thought it was especially admirable that this young woman seemed always to be on top of things, no matter what was happening around her. She seemed unflappable. Mindy's obvious distress, then, was a surprise, *though she is a human being* Esther thought to herself.

Tori was caught unawares. She had never seen this behavior from Mindy, and could not imagine what would make her so upset. She didn't know what to do.

Esther's quiet voice and obvious concern reached something in Mindy's heart, and she came totally undone. The chaos of the studio during the fashion show, the endless travel details of getting their crew to a distant country and back safely and efficiently, or dealing with the prima donnas of the artistic and literary world in New York was easy. Easy, that is, compared to this tenderness that destroyed her defenses and brought a river of tears. Between sobs her story came out in bits and pieces. Something about a two-week vacation ending with her boyfriend telling her he was gay! She was inconsolable.

"You poor dear! What happened? Start from the beginning. David and Arthur aren't paying any attention to us. If they can't find more sports, they'll talk about their Community Center project. If they get hungry, they'll help themselves to turkey sandwiches or some pie."

Mindy drew one last gulping breath and in the tiny voice of a child haltingly began, "I was hurt……no, molested by three neighbor boys… when I was ten or eleven." The women gasped. "Since then, I've been terrified around straight men. The only men I've been comfortable around are gay. They seem kind and safe. You know, Tori, it's why I got involved with fashion—lots of women and mostly gay men! I never told anybody what happened; I didn't know how. Once I tried to confess to a priest, but what was I confessing? I knew the guys had done something very wrong, but I also had heard stuff on TV about women 'asking for it.' How I could have been *asking for it*, I didn't know. But I did know I felt miserably guilty and doomed to hell. The worst part, I realize now, was the silence, keeping it all to myself for so many years."

Esther handed Mindy tissues to give her time to catch her breath before she continued. "I thought Ted was straight. He *said* he was straight, but it makes perfect sense, I guess, why I was attracted to him."

"How did you meet him?" Tori wanted to know.

"He was a teacher's assistant in one of my classes—incredibly charming and well-dressed with an English accent. I was immediately smitten and made a point of going up to him after class and 'chatting him up'. I was so bold! I gave him my phone number, which he very graciously accepted. I remember telling my mom excitedly on the phone that night that I had found the type of man I would eventually marry. A few weeks later I got a call from him inviting me out to dinner. At first I refused, afraid that he might be gay and also afraid that he might be straight. I was a complete mess. I said *no*. A week later he called and invited me out again. I went. Oh Tori, Esther, it was love at first sight. We were drawn to each other like magnets—true soul mates. We've been out together every evening since whenever our schedules permitted, and we were so excited to be planning an adventure to England to visit his parents. He had planned a trip to Egypt long before we met. We hoped to meet up in Malta and fly back to the states together, but he called to say his flight was cancelled and he was flying directly to New York… I should have known something was up. When we finally talked… I don't know…some story about being out late at night walking along the Nile and a guy propositioning him and he said yes!.… and now he knew that being with a man was what he had always wanted!

"Arrghh!…."

The look on Mindy's face as she raised her eyes to the women melted their hearts. Esther continued to ply her with tissues. "We hadn't had sex yet. I guess that should have been a red flag, but I figured he was just being a gentleman and for once I was doing a relationship right. What am I going to do? What is the matter with me?"

This time Esther took Mindy in her arms and rocked her, stroking her hair and wiping her tears. "Mindy, I am so sorry that you were assaulted when you were a child. It is reprehensible. But I want you to know that your angels must have come and protected you during the rape. They protected your soul and accompanied you through the whole event. I want you to stay with me on the farm if you have no work over the holidays. Come and I will love you until you can truly love yourself. That is what this is all about: love. You are totally lovable and never did anything wrong. I want you to believe that and you will see the power *you* have to heal others. Experience is a painful but powerful way to learn lessons, but these lessons never go in vain. You will see how many people you can help because of your direct knowing. All of this is a blessing!"

How could all this have been going on right under my nose? Tori felt like an ostrich taking its head out of the sand. *Exactly how self-centered have I been all this time not to know any of these important details of my friends' lives?* Totally devastated by her assistant's story, her head was spinning from what she had just heard: a powerful tale of pain and trauma, of healing and love. *Where in the world have I been all these years? Was I that lost in my own world, a prisoner of old pain and misunderstanding?* There were events in Tori's life she had not shared with anyone, nor even visited herself for any length of time. *It takes courage to do that, I know, and I confess I have managed to avoid that for most of my life. Maybe someday I'll have Mindy's courage.* She admired this young woman anew.

Chapter 27

AT the refuge of Esther's farm Mindy dove right into the routines of gathering eggs, cleaning stalls, gathering fall apples for applesauce, harvesting winter greens, and keeping bird feeders filled for the hardy ones that stayed the winter. She helped Jack till the summer garden and cover it with a layer of straw. It was Mindy's chance to reconnect with the earth, and she began to relax and enjoy the slow-paced but busy downtime. She was even able to witness the birthing of a foal. In the 200-year-old farmhouse she was treated to Esther's farm-style breakfasts of eggs and homemade bread or scones, and dinners often included winter squash, beets, potatoes, and onions from the garden. Pasture-raised meats were purchased from neighboring farms.

It wasn't long until Jack had her on a horse, which soon became her favorite time. What an amazing feeling to have that connection with such a powerful animal! Of course, Jack made sure to give her the most trustworthy steed, a gentle roan named Daisy. Still shaken by the incident with Breeze, Jack took great care to insure Mindy's safety. He stressed the importance of communication, consistency, and gentleness between horse and rider, teaching her to ride by focusing on body awareness, mindfulness, and breathing.

Mindy spent hours with the horses as she cleaned their stalls, fed and brushed them, and led them to the inside rink for exercise. As she leaned against their warm, rounded bodies, they stood still and absorbed the pain, all the while watching her with large brown eyes as she wept. It was not too long before her soul let down its guard, and her heart broke open.

The responsibility of caring for animals had given Mindy a unique opportunity for personal growth. Esther and Jack trusted her implicitly, as did Arthur, and the horses were powerful in their therapeutic ability. For the first time in her life, she smiled upon awakening and looked forward to the new day. Whole now and balanced with nature, she felt fully alive. There was indeed medicine here, and she hoped that what Esther had taught her was true. Many indigenous cultures refer to "medicine" in a more spiritual way than is usually understood. Native Americans see it *as anything that improves one's connection to the Great Mystery and to all life. It is also anything that brings personal power, strength, and understanding. Horses carry a particularly strong medicine in both their physical and their unearthly power. In shamanic cultural practices throughout the world, Horse enables shamans to fly through the air and reach heaven. Through their special relationship with Horse, the first animal medicine of civilization, humans alter their self-concept beyond measure.*

Maybe living her medicine, Mindy thought, could help other girls who had experienced trauma like hers. Turning down the screeching sound from the intensity of the fashion world had given her time to heal, to rediscover what had heart and meaning in her life. This opportunity to gather land-based wisdom and intuitive knowing exalted her spirit as she took walks around the farm. From now on, she wanted to be a human "BE-ing", not a human "DO-ing".

Winter came with snow and cold and Mindy stayed. Hot chocolate and hours of laughter and reading by the fireplace warmed her body and soul. When the Bernese had a litter, Esther gave Mindy the runt. The two became inseparable, and Esther often wondered who was raising whom. It was beautiful to watch girl and dog romp in the snow, bringing tears of joy to Esther's eyes. Nature had once again done its miraculous job.

Chapter 28

TORI stood in front of her closet, arms *akimbo*. "I don't have a *thing to* wear to yoga class. Just look at this—none of these clothes work for yoga. I can't even move in them. I need something softer, stretchy, and frankly *classier*. I tried that purple exercise outfit they had in the store, but really people there's nothing wrong with looking good while you're doing all these poses, is there?" She knew what she had to do. Still the designer, Tori found her sketch pad and some pencils and soon had her ideas on paper. *I guess I'm not as rusty at this as I thought I might be.* Creating designs was still second nature to her as if hand and brain were joined, and she was pleased with the results that appeared rapidly on the pages. *Now wouldn't it be fun if Anna Mae could come down and help me put these outfits together?* Without hesitation Tori called Anna Mae who was delighted and eager to come visit. Tori smiled with anticipation at the thought of working with her seamstress again and hung up the phone. Glancing at her watch, she exclaimed, "Oh no, late again for yoga class! Is there a message in all this tardiness!"

As she slipped quietly into the yoga studio, the soothing sounds of a sitar and tabla welcomed her. She nodded to her teacher with the customary prayerful greeting of *namaste* and joined the others sitting cross-legged throughout the room. Martha was quietly encouraging the students in her respectful and supportive tone, always so deeply healing to Tori. "That's right, breathe in from the whole abdomen, lift your rib cage, up, up, fill your lungs and then your whole body with good energy. Hold it, and then breathe out, gently, gently, letting go of any stress you may be aware of in your body. Feel it leave the top of your head, the tips of your toes."

Tori felt content. She had never experienced such focus or engagement outside of the fashion industry. Reading about yoga had excited her mind, but performing the asanas and practicing the meditations opened her whole being. *This is exactly what I need to be doing,* she thought, as she settled into her lotus position. When she was in class, she didn't feel tired or stressed. Her recovery from her emotional and physical breakdown had been slow. A month's rest in Old Forge had given her a head start in her healing, but the demands of everyday life didn't always allow for that when she returned home. She was better, but in many ways still frail. Just as the book had promised, though, yoga was healing her. The inner rest was helping her incorporate the benefits of being more *present*, and life had taken on a new glow and meaning. Rain or shine, she never missed a session. In fact, many days she was reluctant to leave and often stayed for a second class.

It seemed like ages before the weekend arrived when Anna Mae, packages in hand, greeted her old boss with a big smile. Tori ushered her in, and soon they were engrossed in conversation as they cut and measured. It was like old times. Tori felt the familiar thrill of handling yards of uncut fabric as the pale lavender and moss green jersey slipped through her fingers. Even if it was just something to wear to yoga class, it still satisfied her need to create something beautiful. The two women bent their heads over the fabric as Anna Mae studied how best to fit the pieces to the pattern.

"How is Mindy?" Anna Mae wanted to know, her mouth full of pins.

"You wouldn't recognize her. You know she's living with Esther now, don't you? Why don't we invite them over for lunch tomorrow?"

"That would be fun. I haven't seen Mindy since she left New York, and it would be so nice to see Esther again. She's been such a dear friend to you."

For a while there was only the whir of the machine as Anna Mae skillfully sewed the outfits. Tori loved that sound. It took her back not only to her studio in New York but to her childhood when she first learned to sew. It was like the background music of her life. Before Tori knew it, Anna Mae was holding up the garments for her approval.

"Thank you, Anna Mae. I couldn't have done this without you."

"Of course you could have, Tori. But it's more fun to do it together, isn't it? Now let's get Esther and Mindy over for a visit!"

The women put together a lovely meal; and when their guests walked in, Anna Mae's eyes opened wide. The change in Mindy was indeed dramatic. Always much too thin, the young woman now stood before her in glowing good health. Her eyes sparkled, and her strong body showed the benefits of an outdoor life.

Hugging and talking all at the same time, the women caught up with each other's news. Esther had lots to tell about her new work with children. She and Mindy were teaching young boys and girls to ride as part of a therapeutic program. They spoke of how heartening it was to see the children's confidence return as they developed trust in these large, gentle animals. Anna Mae's tales of New York City life had them in stitches. As for Mindy, she was full of stories about gardening and cooking, as well as about her favorite horses. She offered to take Anna Mae for a ride.

"No thank you, darling girl. I want to keep these bones I have in good working order, but I can see that it is really working for you."

Esther beamed at her protégé. She could see how much everyone loved this girl, and she was proud of what had been accomplished here. Mindy was like the daughter she had never had, and her pride in her was tangible.

When it came to Tori's turn, she told them about her yoga classes. "Wait 'til you see what Anna Mae and I did yesterday!" She brought out one of the yoga outfits they had made. A chorus of "beautiful!" went round the table, and they meant it: Tori and Anna Mae were definitely a talented team.

"Anna Mae, you should move down here and start a business with Tori. Yoga seems to be the coming thing, and clearly there will be a market for what you two could put together. It would be fabulous!"

Anna Mae smiled fondly at them all. Little did they know that she had been considering a move for some time. This clinched the deal. There was such love and acceptance in this room and great support for each other's well-being. They were all so dear, and how wonderful it would be to have more times such as this.

"Here is dessert, ladies," Tori announced. "And I don't want to hear about diets or the evils of sugar. I never heard of anybody who died of a little piece of chocolate cake. And who could eat that without a scoop of ice cream?"

Later, as they all reluctantly parted, Tori lingered at the door and watched as they drove away, waving until the women were out of sight. A lump caught in her throat when she realized that she couldn't have had these friends without the tutelage of her dear mother-in-law, Dorothy. "Honey, we love the men in our lives, but face it, we get things from our women friends that we never will get from our husbands. Women need each other. Don't ever forget that. Cherish every woman friend you will ever have. You will never regret it."

Interlude, Waving Goodbye

Does it look to you as if I were always waving goodbye? You may recall that I waved goodbye when I left David's hospital room for Malta, when I left the house for Old Forge with Dorothy, and now waving goodbye to friends I realized I had missed. That afternoon when Anna Mae, Esther, and Mindy went home after our little reunion was bittersweet. How wonderful to have us all together, and how wrenching to know that the phrase I used to carelessly throw over my shoulder as I left someone wasn't always true. 'I'll be back before you miss me,' was meant to tell them that there was no need to be sad, yet I hadn't really thought my absence would be hard for anyone. I imagine David missed me, my girls missed me, and friends had missed me. I fully understood this only as I started to get in touch with long-ignored feelings.

It is so much easier to bury your head in the sand when surrounded by nothing but pain and confusion; pretending that everything is okay becomes normal behavior. Numb, you go through the motions of your days, putting on a pretty face and smiling while trying not to feel anything. It sounds so crazy now, but that's how it was for me.

So somebody missed me? That insight revealed itself a layer at a time, like the proverbial peeling of an onion. It took a while and there were tears, as you will see, but opening the heart is a delicate operation. You need skilled hands to help with that, and I will share with you as we go along some of those who had such skill, along with love.

Waving goodbye means letting go of something. Opening the hand to wave is like letting a butterfly drift away from its cocoon and fly away. That makes room for something else, often something better, sometimes even something magical to take its place. Not a bad trade-off, I would say.

When you outgrow a dress, give it away; don't clutter up your closet. Buy or make or design a new one. When you outgrow what no longer fits in your life, gently let that go, too. Your option then can be to design a new one, crafted just for you. You will see.

Chapter 29

For the second time this week, Tori's yoga teacher mentioned something she wanted them to remember. *I need to write that down so I won't forget it again,* Tori told herself, and she thought of the journal she had begun during her sojourn in Old Forge with Dorothy. As soon as she got home, she searched for the book and found it behind a cushion in her sitting room. The soft green cover felt good in her hands, warming her heart to the memories of that time. Opening to the first page, she scanned the notes she had made on her visit to the astrologer one chilly autumn afternoon. Dawn's card was still there, and on impulse she called the number and made a phone appointment for the following week.

Who knew less than a year ago that I would be taking yoga classes and consulting an astrologer? Tori marveled at the changes in her life. She was reading *Siddhartha, Play of Consciousness, Bhagavad Gita,* the *Lives of Yogis,* books on feminism, the poetry of Khalil Gibran, a textbook of yoga psychology, even the Kabbalah—anything and everything that related to a change in consciousness. It was curious to her that in school reading had been so difficult. These new interests, however, were grabbing her attention, and somehow it made reading easier for her.

Tori's reading material was not the only departure for her. Her appearance also reflected her new outlook as she dressed to please herself rather than the public. With most of her jewelry and make-up gone, her clothes were simpler but still becoming, and she wore her hair in a more casual style that did not require hair spray. This was a departure for the elegant, sleek, perfectly coiffed and bejeweled fashion designer of New York City. She still loved color and design, but in general her loose skirts and flats indicated the greater ease she was feeling with herself and with the world.

The change in Tori did not go unnoticed, and the people at the country club wondered if her new behavior had anything to do with the breakdown she had suffered. She ran into a club acquaintance at the store one day; and when she asked Tori how she was, she answered, "Fabulous! I've been taking yoga classes and have never felt better." The woman refrained awkwardly from asking what it was. Noticing the woman's hesitation she continued on, "You should come. I think it would really be good for you. Yoga is so healthy for everybody." Awkward silence again. Finally, her acquaintance demurred. "Tori, but I'm just so busy right now, but maybe lunch someday at the club?" Tori watched her wander on down the aisle, disappointed that her good news was not well-received, and the implied judgment stung. Why did she care so much what others thought of her? She would have to get over that if she was going to continue on this path!

In class the next day her yoga teacher asked Tori if she wanted to join a group that was going to see Ram Butler. This man had just come back from India after studying with a swami there. He wanted to tell people about his guru, Swami Muktananda, Head of the Siddha lineage who would be coming to America soon. Tori jumped at the chance.

That evening at the Convocation Hall the pungent scene of incense infused the air; and the crowd moved to the familiar sounds of Indian music Tori had come to love, creating a festive atmosphere. This was all new to her: monks in orange robes, college students, bearded devotees in loose white pants wearing strings of beads around their necks, young women in long cotton dresses with flowers in their hair. Everyone was here to learn about this holy man. There were the strains of the guitar Ram Butler played, and many in the crowd joined in the chant that was being sung. Something important, something joyous was happening here. When the speaker began to talk about his experiences with the Swami, a hush fell over the crowd. It was fascinating to Tori, and she could not get enough of the stories he was telling. At once humbled and thrilled, Tori felt—almost like a bolt of lightning—that her whole life was forever being transformed.

This is not something I remember experiencing before, yet it seems vaguely familiar. I wonder why that is? She felt connected to all the people there, and pure joy descended on her. In that moment she thought of Luca; and for the first time, it was with peace, not worry. Wherever he was, she knew he was all right.

Chapter 30

TORI felt overwhelmed when she returned home from the convocation. The heady experience she had there met the daily frustrations and distractions of home life, and she felt pulled between two worlds. How to balance these worlds, how to experience the divine and still "chop wood and carry water" as a Chinese Zen master wrote in his poem a thousand years ago, was not easy. Her mind and heart felt scattered to the winds.

While sitting at a traffic light in such a state, the mantra Martha had taught them in class appeared in the midst of her mind's chatter: *Om Shanti, Shanti Om*. She began to say it over and over until a sense of calm was restored. She drew a deep breath and looked around, as if she wouldn't be surprised to see a magician standing there. But it wasn't magic, she knew. It was the power of the words connecting to her core, ancient words that had guided many souls to a happier and more serene life. Tori smiled and made a note to remember this. *You are what you think!*

Still, she sighed as she mulled over the rejections from some of the people she knew, and it made her feel even more of an outcast. The way she dressed, the way she entertained, and now delving into something as foreign as yoga was just too much for them.

Often even David was on the fence about this passion of hers. These days the tiniest thing could throw her off balance as she was still not strong and stable enough to absorb his criticisms. He often looked disapprovingly at her intense devotion to her yoga practice, and his friends didn't help. They filled his head with stories of cults and crazy people in robes. "What if she runs off with one of those? Then you won't have anyone to cook your dinner every night!" His fears were further fueled by the story of the Jonestown Massacre, where the leader's followers drank Kool-Aid in a suicide pact. When Tori heard those arguments, she was angry and frustrated. *Can't I have my own life?*

Later that month Martha again invited Tori to a gathering, this time to meet the man Ram Butler had told them about, his guru Swami Muktananda. He would be at the ashram. Not only could they meet him in person, they could also receive his Darshan, a blessing.

Without hesitation, Tori told her *yes.*

On the way home, Tori thought about what she would tell David. She still hadn't had the conversation with him about the channeling with Dawn. At that time Dawn had told Tori that she and David shared a deep love, but they needed to communicate better. *I'll tell him soon.*

Arriving home, she called David to tell him of her plans. He did not take it well. "I don't want you up there. Who knows what they might be up to? Frankly, Tori, from what I hear these days, I don't trust those people. Oh, and I will be home a little early; I have a meeting tonight. Can you get dinner ready early?"

Tori began to do a slow burn as she hung up the phone. *What could be harmful or threatening to him if I want to go meet a yogi? Her teacher was totally trustworthy; David had even met her once—she certainly wouldn't put anyone in danger. This is a holy man, not a criminal!*

As the larger picture formed in her mind, she began to tremble. Unbidden thoughts and revelations swirled around her like an ominous cloud. The more she thought, the angrier she became. *I have a life, too, don't I? Who does he think he is to tell me I can't go? He can just make a sandwich for dinner.*

Tori stormed out of the house, her eyes fiery and her jaw set. She didn't look back as she jerked open the door of her car and flung herself into the seat, thrusting the key into the ignition. Fired up, literally and figuratively, Tori's foot found the gas pedal, and the car screeched out of the driveway. *God help me, I can't believe I'm doing this.* She hesitated only a moment before choosing the route that led to Dorothy's.

Interlude, Finding Meditation Space

This was such a difficult time. David and I had so much to be thankful for together, but our lives shone with different lights. He was a darling of the community, and rightly so; while I was delegated to running the house, taking care of the girls, and fitting in my spiritual practice whenever I could.

I remember waking one night at 3:00 a.m. and having trouble getting back to sleep, so I decided to get up to meditate while the household was still. The room that I used for this, the playroom, was small and always in order—a cozy space. There was a chair in there that worked perfectly for sitting in lotus position, and I couldn't wait to settle in.

That time of night is considered a "magic time" when the veil is very thin and spirit can speak softly to one's being if they are awake. Baba said it was 'God's time'. Meditation had not come easy for me; but given enough time and practice, it was becoming more familiar, and I was ready to listen to what spirit had to say.

My body relaxed into the soft cushion, and I began the short chant that leads to the inner silence I was looking forward to. Just then, the doorknob turned, and David peered into the room. "Oh, there you are! I woke up and couldn't find you. Come back to bed before you get cold." He turned around, never asking what I was doing, or if he was interrupting.

Words rose up in me, but I didn't let them boil over. The peace I had begun to feel had been shattered, and the magic moment had passed. I uncurled my legs and slowly stood up. Yes, it was cool in the room, but I wasn't cold. I knew he just didn't understand; but if I didn't go back to bed, he would be back again, this time angry and impatient. I couldn't face that, not tonight, not the short, clipped commands; it was better just to go back to bed.

When am I going to have my own space, I wondered, as I slowly began to travel down the hall? For a brief time I had been in my own world, and the journey back was not one I wanted to make so precipitously.

"Are you coming?"
"Yes, I'll be there in a minute."
Back in bed I pulled up the covers and lay immobile. How can I reconcile

this situation: how can I be a good wife, a good mother, and still be true to what I know I must do? Then I remembered the mantra that means peace: Om Shanti, Shanti Om. It helped quiet my mind as I silently said the words over and over until they allowed me some rest.

Chapter 31

Her car idled for a moment in Dorothy's driveway while she considered how she could possibly confide with her mother-in-law about her own son. *Oh dear! She'll think I'm a complete lunatic or that I hate her son?*

Tori found Dorothy sitting in her favorite chair with her knitting. Dorothy, always pleased to see her daughter-in-law, was immediately aware that things were amiss. Tori's sudden visit and demeanor could only mean there was trouble since it was not like her to show up without notice. "Dear, it's *so* good to see you. Have you eaten? Is everything all right?"

"Well, I think I ate at some point today, but I don't know for sure! I am not really hungry. I guess I could eat something. Is that peach cobbler cooling on the sill? Bless you for your hospitality and generosity.... always!"

Dorothy knew that any problem could be solved better over a cup of tea and maybe a nice piece of pie or *babka*.

"Well, follow me and let's get you some tea and pie and then we'll talk."

Tori's heart loosened as they began to talk and the tension soon dissolved into tears. Words tumbled over one another in their eagerness to tell the story, until finally she was forced between the tears and the words to pause and take a breath. Dorothy looked at her with tenderness. "How can I help, dear?"

The words were out of Tori's mouth before she could consider them.

"I need to go to the ashram, and I want you to go with me. Please don't think I am crazy! David doesn't want me to go, but I thought maybe if *you* went along..."

"David will get over it, just give him some time," Dorothy advised. "But you must call him and tell him where you are. And I *will* go to the ashram with you." Dorothy was an Orthodox woman, but she was a kind and generous mother-in-law and was happy to oblige her daughter-in-law's occasional eccentricities. She saw it mainly as a chance to spend some time with Tori and really find out what was going on.

As it turned out, the ashram was in the heart of the area where

Orthodox rabbis and families gathered during the summer. During the years to come, many rabbis would request an audience with Baba whenever he was there.

Tori went to the phone and called home, as Dorothy suggested, with some trepidation. She told David matter-of-factly where she was, and that she and his mother were going to the ashram the next day. She was surprised that the tension she heard in his voice when he answered the phone disappeared, and with sincere gentleness he wished them both a safe trip.

Chapter 32

EVERY day is a new day. Sometimes there is a day that makes us feel so wonderful, so perfect that we want to capture it and hold it forever like a wonderful dream. When that happens, we wonder why each day can't be like that, but there are so many answers to that question.

Tori thought back to her discovery of *Yoga, Youth, and Reincarnation*. She had an instant experience akin to discovering gold by the time she was four pages in. So impressed with what she was reading, she bought copies for Anna Mae and Mindy in New York, as well as for other friends and family. Would this event she and Dorothy were headed for turn out to be like that discovery, too?

The weather was perfect, and they rolled down the car windows to enjoy the sweet summer smells wafting from the fields and woods they passed. "Remember this, Mother? Kyle used to be at camp here, and one summer David had to come get her when she was sick. He picked her up and headed straight for Old Forge, and she was well in two days. We always call it our healing place."

As they neared the turnoff to the ashram where people had come from far and near to welcome this holy man, Tori turned to Dorothy. "Are you ready for this?"

Her mother-in-law answered with a smile. "As long as I'm with you, Tori, everything's fine."

The parking lot was dusty, and license plates reflected how far people had come. The size of the crowd was astonishing to Tori. *I guess this is bigger than I thought,* she marveled as she guided Dorothy through the swarm. They were greeted with warm smiles and asked if this was their first meeting with Baba Muktananda. They nodded and were directed to the *Darshan* shop to purchase a small offering for the guru, which represented an exchange of energy. They chose some strawberries, incredibly red and fragrant, and proceeded with anticipation and excitement to their seats.

When Tori had attended the yoga convocation earlier, Ram Butler spoke of a guru everyone wanted to see. He explained that he had not wanted a guru for himself, but he knew that this man was truly different.

Swami Muktananda was a perfected master, a *Sod Guru*, who had been given the power to bestow grace through transference of divine energy. Tori had listened that night in wondrous fascination and confusion. She hoped meeting the Swami would bring clarity.

Before she could entertain another thought, a conch shell was blown, the sound of it electrifying the country air. A powerful hush following its call was broken by the drone of harmoniums, and the chant to the light, Ariti, began. For the next hour and a half, Dorothy and Tori sat as they listened to the devotional Sanskrit texts honoring the universal guru, the teacher, the light that vanishes the darkness in the world.

Tori was filled with peace and ease, and she wept tears of joy. As if in a waking dream, she glided through the rest of the afternoon: waiting in a long line, putting their offering in a basket and then bowing down to Baba, feeling the soft touch of a peacock feather on her head.

On the way home Dorothy told Tori that she watched her go into a very deep meditation. "I didn't bow down myself when I met Baba, because I didn't know what that meant; but it was interesting to me. I could tell it touched you very deeply, my dear. Your face was just shining."

Tori hadn't remembered that, but she did know something profound had occurred. She reached over and pressed Dorothy's hand. "It did touch me, and I can't think of anyone I would rather share this day with. Thank you for coming."

They were quiet the rest of the way home, but in the deepest part of herself Tori knew that something had irrevocably been set. She could hardly wait for the next opportunity to explore further this path that was so new, yet also so familiar in some deep recesses of her being.

Interlude, Beginning Siddha Yoga

When I arrived for my first weekend at the permanent ashram they had built for Baba Muktananda, I stepped into a world I had hardly imagined. The pure beauty of the grounds instantly drew me in: the peaceful expanse of verdant lawns, and rose gardens surrounded by lovely old oaks and evergreens. I felt my shoulders relax, and the rest of my body followed. Someone had told me once to be where you were most comfortable. They could have been describing this place.

After dinner there was a meditation. Devotees, as well as those attending for the first time, converged from all directions. Just beyond the entrance to the building there was a small room where people left their shoes before they went in to meditate. This represented leaving the 'ego' at the door, and it was interesting to see who had trouble with this ritual and who did not. Obediently, I slipped out of my shoes and turned the corner into the great hall. At the sight of the splendor of it all, I stopped to take it in: an altar decorated with flowers and small statuettes, lit candles everywhere, the prevailing aroma of incense. There was a turquoise rug with a floral pattern, and Swarovski crystal chandeliers honoring the Shakti that twinkled above like diamonds. Large pictures of Bidi Baba Nityananda commanded the walls, seeming to compel us to devotion. Gurumayi was resplendent in her orange robes occupying a chair that was itself a work of art. For someone like me who was so attuned to color and design, it was especially stunning. I could hardly speak, but I didn't need to.

Music filled the hall as people moved rapturously to the sound of Om Namah Shivaya intoning over and over. There was comfortable seating in the back for those who needed it, but I found an unoccupied meditation pillow and assumed a lotus position. Soon my body resonated with the chanting and music, and I became one with the rhythms around me.

I hardly remembered the talk that followed. Getting used to this whole new way of worshipping and finding a way to God was an eye-opener and very different from my Orthodox upbringing. But over time I learned that it was a way to my own Self. That Self had been buried for a long time under mounds of emotional debris, and it was good to finally find her again.

Nikki Friedlander

After the talk that first night, the chant of Hari Krishna with everyone clapping and swaying was absolutely joyous. When I walked back to my sleeping quarters, I was dazzled by the stars, by what I had just seen and heard. Life continued to awaken to me to another glorious part of myself.

Interlude, Luca in India

Sitars and harmoniums played and incense burned non-stop as Luca listened to his new friends, Richard and Michael, sing the praises of their new guru. Luca's hair now fell far below his shoulders, and his beard and gaunt frame made him look like the Indian sadhus. Richard and Michael teased that he had the 'fashion' of a saint; now he just needed to finish the inside job! They assured him that his experience in Manila was not due to trauma and exhaustion. Instead, it had been the well-earned enlightenment that their guru could better explain.

Luca's heart was wide open; he continued to weep uncontrollably for months. The terror-the glory; the pain-the ecstasy; the Love, always the Love; it all made him weep. God was everything or God was nothing, and he chose everything. Whatever it took, however long it took, he would devote himself in service to God and his guru. Eventually he learned the guru is his very self.

First, he must learn to meditate to control his breathing and his thoughts. Yoga and the asanas came next, with daily classes held mid-day in the meditation room of the ashram. Finally, there was the practice of selfless service for the sick, dying, and starving of the world. It was a sublime time for Luca, and not once did he consider returning to New York. The city now appeared shallow and materialistic to him, the pinnacle of greed and consumption. Though he admired the history of his native Malta, he much preferred India, a country reeking of God and spiritual strivings. What money meant to Americans, God meant to Indians, and he couldn't get enough. Vogue? Tori? He didn't want to judge, but he bowed his head in deep gratitude to Sean for keeping him from that path.

Luca had found, with the help of his friends, a kutir or cave-like hut in which to meditate and practice chanting 'Ram, Ram, Ram' until the guru returned to town.

Months passed until Luca was called back to the ashram. It was with great excitement mixed with trepidation that he first gazed upon Muktananda, Sean's guru, and he was not disappointed. Before him stood an exquisite, lithe, dark-skinned man with the gestures of a courtesan. His bright white teeth, sun glasses, and woolen caps created a 'movie star' image for this most perfectly realized being.

Baba was a siddha, which in India means a being in complete union with absolute consciousness. There was great blessing just from being in his presence. Luca could feel it, and he wept for the last time for himself and instead experienced deep compassion for the unrealized path. He felt at home with his new father, his Baba, understood and forgiven. He felt unconditional love, and he knew he was changed. God lives within you as you, he was taught, and it is your birthright to experience this daily. With this guidance, Luca would come to the full realization of his divinity.

Luca did not contact his family or anyone in America for many years. When he did, he discovered that he and Sean had been captured when their plane had been shot down in Viet Nam, and that only he had survived the POW camp. Sean was 'missing' for a decade before his family declared him officially dead. Luca's family prayed daily for him, unwilling to close the door on the possibility of his return. Their prayers would not go unanswered.

Chapter 33

SPEEDING down the road, Tori gripped the wheel of her car and stared straight ahead with a determination fueled by long-standing anger. That last scene with David was *absolutely* the last straw. So what if she forgot to pick up his favorite blue suit at the cleaner's? Did that make her a bad person? And it wasn't as if he didn't have other suits to wear. Since when was this man such a clothes horse?

The situation this morning had gotten out of hand as he berated her, once again erupting verbally like a volcano, and she heard her voice, steely and focused, "That's it, David. I'm outa here." She hadn't even looked back, but she could imagine him standing there, slack-jawed in mid-sentence. There was a moment of panic before she told herself to just head to the lawyer's office, except she couldn't remember where his office was! The streets looked all the same in her state of confusion; and then, as if it had a mind of its own, the car turned onto the road that led to Esther's house. She recognized it at once and realized that whatever guidance had intervened, she was *indeed* going in the right direction. She breathed a deep sigh of relief.

"Esther, what am I going to do?" Tori blurted out when her friend opened her beautifully carved front door. Esther took in the situation with a practiced eye and led Tori to the kitchen. "Let's have some tea and you can tell me what's going on."

"Oh, Esther, I don't know, I reached a point this morning when I realized I just couldn't take it anymore. You know how David can be. He's so charming when he's at the community center or with his clients. But he's just Mr. Volcano at home, and I'm tired of it! He can't have a normal conversation if I forget something, and he thinks I spend too much time and money at the ashram. He just doesn't get it. I was on my way to the lawyer when I got confused, and the car seemed to turn itself down your road by itself. And here I am."

Always the steady port in Tori's storms, Esther listened to her friend's story and advised her to see a therapist before she took any action. "You might remember that I saw someone after my disastrous first marriage. I can't tell you how helpful that was."

Tori was taken aback. How could she have forgotten about the turmoil Esther had endured with her first husband? Esther and Arthur had been happily married for such a long time now, it was hard to remember Esther not contented in marriage.

"Just don't do anything drastic right now, Tori. Let things simmer down and give your head a chance to clear. Seeing someone will help you look at the whole situation. After that, you'll know what to do."

Tori did listen and slowly calmed down as she realized that her wise friend was right. Feeling stronger, she stood up and gave Esther a hug. Words weren't necessary as they stepped back from each other, and Tori gave her old friend a smile before she turned and walked out the door. On the front porch she stopped to look out at the rolling fields with gentle horses grazing there and let the peace of it all enter her heart.

Chapter 34

"Burn them?"

"That's exactly what I said; burn them!! Your mother can't hurt you now. You are writing what you wished you could have said to her long ago. Those words have been stuck in your throat for a long time. You have written the words and spoken them out loud; and now it is time to get rid of them forever!"

The therapist went on more gently. "Tori, that little girl lived in your heart and had to be given her voice; you bravely allowed her to speak, and now that she has expressed herself you can burn what was written. It will free you both, and that little girl will be integrated into the whole of you. You will see. It is amazingly healing."

Tori would never have thought that writing a letter to her mother could help, but the therapist was right. The old thoughts and feelings of being unwanted and unloved that had tormented her since childhood still rose unbidden at the oddest times and seemed to have a power of their own. Early in her marriage, Tori felt surprised and even frightened when David had his daily eruptions. She didn't know how to respond and often stood like a deer in headlights while he directed his rage at her. Now that she understood more about his pain, it all began to make sense. When people talked about their *baggage*, she thought of the knot of anger and grief she had been carrying around for so long. She knew exactly how they felt, and it was time to set it down and free herself and David.

It had taken a number of weeks to get around to this assignment from Elaine. *How was this going to help anything?* Each time she sat down with pen and paper, she was soon up again, distracted by the ringing of a telephone, a knock at the door, or an errand that she had forgotten to run. Finally it was something she witnessed in a store that made her realize she couldn't put it off any longer. It happened while she was out shopping for some new napkins. A middle-aged woman and presumably her teenage daughter were in the next aisle over, and Tori couldn't help but overhear their conversation. "That's a horrible color for you. You would have to pick out the most expensive thing in the store. Why do you need to go to the prom, anyway? You couldn't even get a date by yourself. What do you know about this boy?"

Tori whispered to herself, *that was me.* It tore at her heart. She wanted to go over and say something, but she knew the girl would be embarrassed and the woman would be incensed. Instead, she tried the exercise Elaine had taught her: put light around them and say a prayer. She left the store and went home, put her purchases on the dining room table, and went straight to her desk while the experience and her emotions were fresh.

The first voice she heard was of herself as a three-year-old child who was always in trouble and didn't know why. As she wrote, she felt very small; her fingers were not big enough for the pencil she was using. She was amazed that such a little person had such an enormous amount of grief, and the scrawls across the paper were a measure of the confusion and hurt she had experienced at that tender age.

Dearest Mommy, why don't you like me? I try to be good. That was all she could bear to put on paper, but the message carried all that she needed to say. Tears wet her cheeks as she put the pencil down. For the first time, she let them flow uninterruptedly from the depth of that abandonment and the futility of her efforts to be reclaimed.

Her second letter was written in her teenage voice after the visit from angels in the middle of the night. They had appeared in her bedroom waking her to the sound of strange voices, speaking a language she had never heard. As she became more alert, she discovered to her amazement that she could understand them. *We are here to guide you, dear child, through your growing awareness and spiritual development. Do not be afraid. We will always be around you. You can call on us at any time.* Comforting as the message was from the angels, it only proved to exacerbate her sense of isolation. Who could she confide in about this event that overwhelmed her? No one would believe her, and she would feel even more like an alien from another planet. Her fingers gripped the pen as she thought of all the ways she had been thwarted in her attempts to be loved and accepted. It was distressful to re-live the isolation and profound loneliness of that young woman. *No one, there had really been no one.*

Tori sat up tall at her desk, a *frisson* passing up her spine. She was pushing the paper away and then drawing it closer, when she heard what sounded like a whisper loudly filling the room. *Love....Forgiveness.* Her body was filled with a rush of supreme calm. How hard it had been, and how simple understanding those words was now. She *could* be free, not by asking anything of her mother, but by asking this only of herself: to heal her troubled childhood through love and forgiveness. *Mother, I do forgive you. You did all you knew how to do.*

This time her tears began in earnest. They flowed for a long time, backward into that dark misery that had been hers, and then forward into the light that awaited anyone willing to take this journey. Loving herself no longer depended upon anything external. It was all about accepting the beautiful and whole person that she was: a spiritual being having a human experience. She now had the key!

Tori got up then from the desk in the alcove and looked out into the quiet street. The sun that flooded the room when she began writing these letters now hovered on the horizon, and the first faint star appeared in the pale sky above. The relief she felt spread throughout the room until quietly, but with authority, joy enveloped her and chased away any shadows that remained.

She closed the drapes, moving deliberately, mindfully, and with gratitude—the way she would later offer up her evening prayers before going to bed. She retrieved the letters from her desk and took them with her as she lit a small fire in the grate. Quietly she blessed them as she placed them on the sputtering flames, one at a time, and watched as they caught and then quickly turned to ash, sending small smoke signals to the universe.

One night I dreamed I was walking along the beach with the Lord. Many scenes from my life flashed across the sky.

In each scene I noticed footprints in the sand. Sometimes there were two sets of footprints, other times there was one only.

This bothered me because I noticed that during the low periods of my life, when I was suffering from anguish, sorrow or defeat, I could see only one set of footprints, so I said to the Lord,

"You promised me Lord, that if I followed you, you would walk with me always. But I have noticed that during the most trying periods of my life there has only been one set of footprints in the sand. Why, when I needed you most, have you not been there for me?"

The Lord replied, "The years when you have seen only one set of footprints, my child, is when I carried you."

Mary Stevenson, 1936

Interlude, Going back to David

I went back home after that. It was not only the work with my therapist, but also the teachings at the ashram that led me to a deeper understanding of love, of its vagaries and comforts and its ultimate saving grace. In turn, David had written to me; and if you will bear with me, I would like to share his letter with you.

'You are right in what you say. You have been an extraordinary support to anything I have ever done. I could not have had a more loving and caring wife and partner. Much of what you did made me look a lot better than I would otherwise have looked. I know this. I have always appreciated and admired your actions toward me and in the manner you carried yourself. I have always been in a hurry and have not taken the time to slow down and let it all happen by itself. I am not in a hurry any more since I have everything I ever wanted. I only want to be happy and serene and loving and caring and take each day as it comes.

I am again excited about working and know that the fruits of my labor will be there even if I slow down and work in a more relaxed manner.

I truthfully became frightened these past five years that my business would keep reducing to nothingness and I would have less and less each year. I became subservient to the customer and let them get the upper hand. The more I tried to please the customer and bend over backwards and let him misuse me, the more irritated I became and the more I resented having to serve him. I thought I was acting as a professional, but I was not being treated as a professional; and even though my customers were being taken care of with extra service, they did not show the respect I was looking for. I realize now that I will do my job and treat these people fairly, but I will be in control and will not be subservient any longer.

I am not going to be married to my business any longer but will now use it as it should be used—just a vehicle to make a living. I am able to make serious money without the pressure.

Tori, I love you with all my heart and want what you want. I love being with you and don't need anyone else. I want to have fun and laugh and enjoy our life together. There is no one else out there.

I know that you needed some space and I can appreciate that even though I do get a bit lonesome for you.

Your letter was beautiful and well put. I have read it five times and I feel every thought that you described. I know how you feel and I am thankful that you took the time to put it into words. I have never meant to be difficult on purpose and I have never wanted to hurt you. I have had a bad time because I let myself get out of control. Hopefully that will not happen again to me.

I would hope we can spend our lives loving each other and caring for each other and respecting each other and enjoying our girls together. This is the most important exercise that I would want for the future. Yes, it's a new year and I will do everything in my power to be worthy of your love and be your friend. I want you to be my friend, Tori, forever and ever.'

I cherish that letter. It was always so difficult for him to express his feelings, and so this is uniquely precious. Sometimes, I know, it is easier to communicate at a bit of a distance. There is no fear of being interrupted, of having old issues come up, when you can speak simply and from the heart to a piece of paper. I know it was more comfortable for him, and I accepted that.

Of course, it was not exactly 'happily ever after' from that time on; but enough had been cleared away that we understood each other better, and a certain level of respect that I felt had been lacking was evident. He did love me. I did love him. It was as simple, and as profound, as that.

Chapter 35

LIFE took on a new rhythm after Tori and David made their amends. Their basic characters did not change, but their way of being with each other improved. David became more comfortable with Tori's devotion to her spiritual practice, especially after he made several trips to the ashram with her. On one occasion there was an opportunity to meet Baba, and Tori persuaded her husband to come with her. After they had gone through the routines of discarding shoes, sitting during the meditation, and finally meeting Baba, Tori introduced him to the holy man. Baba looked at David and said through his interpreter, "He is a good man."

Another visit was not as pleasant, but David was a good sport. They were to stay overnight, and she had forgotten to make a reservation at the hotel the ashram had purchased. Ending up in a summer cabin, with no heat, in late October, in the mountains, and only one twin bed did not make for a comfortable night; but he didn't complain. He did have something to say, however, about how Baba gave him *shaktipat*, the conferring of spiritual energy. "Boy! He pulled my head back, pulled my ears, rubbed my hair, poked my eyes, and swatted me with the peacock feather. I guess he wanted to make sure I got it! I'm going out now for lunch. See you when the program ends."

Tori didn't tell him she had silently encouraged Baba to *give it to him, wake him up!* She couldn't help but laugh.

Tori couldn't wait to tell Esther about all the things she was doing and learning. "Wouldn't you like to come sometime? I know you're always busy with the farm and the dogs, but I'd love to have some company up there." To her surprise Esther agreed. It was true that she was busy, but loyalty and support for friends came before chores. She had seen so many positive changes in Tori that she knew something good must be going on. Admittedly, she had worried for a while; they *all* had. After the breakdown Tori seemed a bit *too* enthused about her yoga classes; and when she dove into the ashram thing headfirst, Esther had to allay David's fears that one day he would come home to a wife with a shorn head and orange robes! Tori and David were actually doing much better. Theirs was a pretty spicy relationship—that wasn't going to change! But Esther had observed frequent spontaneous moments of tenderness between them, and Tori's judgments and complaints had almost completely subsided.

The new clothes and the hairstyle Tori adopted were certainly a change from her city fashion designer days, and the literature she was reading could definitely be described as a bit *offbeat*. Regardless, Esther admired her friend's spiritual focus, and accompanying her to the ashram would maintain their already close bond.

The day for the excursion to the ashram came quickly; and Esther, although she had visited numerous temples and churches, ranked the ashram and its grounds among the most lovely she had ever visited. The place had a palpable peace that disarmed and drew her in. No wonder Tori loved it so. She took it in as Tori proudly showed her around the lush gardens, the lake, the small temple and the meditation hall where devotees sat draped in shawls as they chanted to the drone of the harmoniums. Esther's place of devotion, outside of her synagogue, had always been nature; and this ashram surprisingly captured her heart in an unexpected way. This place could indeed heal and was grounding for Tori—that is what she had been noticing. It was of benefit for Tori; and perhaps, she thought, it could also be beneficial for herself. How long had it been since she had taken time for her own spiritual rejuvenation? Smiling broadly to Tori, she laughed as she declared, *sign me up*!

Interlude, Leaving the Ashram

I didn't know for a long time why I wanted to take part in these spiritual activities. I do know that I loved ceremony; and in my mind, all is ceremony. Even setting the table for dinner at night, selecting the placemats and napkins, honoring the food, the people at the table, the husband who worked hard to make it possible to have a good life; all of this was part of ceremony. To my mind, it was part of the grand design of the master designer of the universe.

I did love the ceremonies at the ashram as they were such an integral part of the whole experience for me; so it was a natural progression to create an altar in my home. That way I could incorporate the puja into my daily life. After I decided a corner of my sitting room would be the perfect location to set it up, I went searching for just the right table to hold the articles I would need. I headed, of course, to my favorite consignment store. They carried only high-end furnishings at reasonable prices; and I knew if I told them what I wanted, they would call me as soon as something suitable was in stock. As it turned out, they already had just what I had in mind, but this seemed to happen all the time for me. Once I decided on something I wanted, it seemed to be just waiting for me at a store. I only had to utter the desire.

Once home I assembled the candles and incense, the picture of the guru, a set of little bells, and some fresh flowers on the small round table situated underneath a mirror in a gold frame. I stepped back to observe the configuration and declared it perfect. When David came home, I showed him what I had arranged, and he agreed that it indeed was beautiful. There was no negative comment, we had made peace with this a long time ago. The next morning, I was ready to do my first ceremony. Reverently I lit the candle, in this way adding one more light to the world. That is the image I always have whenever I see a candle that is sending up its flame. Then I began to say the words I knew, not just from rote but from the heart:

> Hail the True Guru
> Om, salutations to the guru, who
> is shiva! His form is Being,
> Consciousness, and Bliss. He
> is transcendent, calm, free

from all support, and luminous.
Salutations to the goddess
who's emerging and rescuer
from the cycle of birth and death,
who has assumed a body to meet
the needs of her devotees, and
whose nature is consciousness
and being.

And then I said the Gaytreye Mantra:
Oh God! Thou art the Giver of Life,
Remover of pain and sorrow,
The Bestower of happiness,
Oh! Creator of the Universe.
May we receive thy supreme sin-destroying light,
May thou guide our intellect in the right direction.
And after that, I burned the incense and rang the bells.

Rituals like this, when done with love and honor, can expand one's awareness of the divine. When time is set aside to go inward and be aware of the connection to all, one's consciousness cannot help but expand. I loved getting up in the morning and waving incense and lighting the candles and saying the prayers and chants. To honor the gurus was the perfect way for me to start the day. In the evening when I snuffed out the candles and said prayers, it seemed to put the perfect cap on whatever the day had brought. I also noticed that I was in charge of time in my life. Amazing! Anything I did was without effort.

This ritual has sustained me through so many years, so many challenges, so many joys. It is so familiar that it almost seems as if it is my breath now, a part of me that emerges each day from my deepest being. And each time I always remember to say 'thank you'.

The ashram became my other home for some years, almost as much as Old Forge, as I participated in intensives on many weekends and spent a month there each summer. I even wore saris while I was there festooned with the jewelry I had again collected. David and I did argue, I admit, about the money I spent, and about my donating an expensive ring so I could help support the place. He did not worry any longer about the spiritual aspects, as he had in the beginning.

As they say, to everything there is a season. A spiritual journey has many twists and turns, and it is individual for each person. Only one's own experience can be the most meaningful, not what the person on your left or right might *be responding to. It took years of study and practice to realize what was taking place inside me, but it always felt right; Siddha Yoga gave me what I needed then. In time that would change, of course, but being shown the way to my own divine self was priceless, and the growth I found in that was the strength of my own character.*

Chapter 36

"Mom, it's a girl. You have a granddaughter!"

The early morning phone call woke Tori, groggy with sleep, but her daughter's voice brought her wide awake.

Tori recalled the event as if it was yesterday, and it still brought tears to her eyes. Her life, her thoughts, even her identity had experienced an immediate shift when her daughter became a mother and she became a grandmother. *Grandma, Nana.* The words rolled off her tongue like honey, and her heart swelled with such pride and joy her body could hardly contain them.

David had been equally excited. He had looked forward to being a grandparent probably as much as Tori. The lineage would continue, and introducing each new family member to Old Forge with a ride in the little red boat was a rite of passage the grandchildren would always remember. It was one of David's favorite memories, too.

The focus for Tori and David shifted with the birth of their first grandchild, and there were more grandbabies to come. A softening happened *between* them and *inside* of each of them during this period. Was it age? Was it acceptance?

The activities at the ashram still drew Tori in on occasion, but not with the same passion they had when her life was in turmoil. She did continue her Siddha yoga studies via a correspondence course written by Ram Butler, which she read for fifteen years. She even carried it with her in a little suede purse fashioned for that purpose. And, of course, she maintained her morning and evening prayers and her puja that she would pray before as long as she had breath.

Flower of Life

Tori was always open to spiritual growth and intrigued when a friend encouraged her to attend a *Flower of Life* workshop. The teacher who walked into the classroom carried an aura about him that was positively captivating. Drunvelo Melchizedek's demeanor was unlike anyone's she had met before. It was completely devoid of ego, and his casual and often humorous teaching style was a delight and so necessary for the intense material he had decided to impart. He had garnered his wisdom directly from 70 shamans and tribes the world over. When he began to speak about humans losing their memory 13,000 years ago at the fall of Atlantis, and then told them about his travels for seventeen years with a blue and a green angel that were part of him, Tori's eyes opened wide.

Drunvelo also talked about cellular memory, and she thought back to an experience she had some time ago. In the middle of the night, she felt the earth shaking and woke David. "We're having an earthquake!"

"Don't be silly, just go back to sleep," was his unconcerned response.

Tori couldn't go back to sleep, though; and the next morning they found out that an earthquake had actually been recorded in the Adirondack mountains. Later that morning, she called Robert Mahany after she began to shake as if she had had 100 cups of coffee, which of course she hadn't. His explanation was that the real earthquake had triggered a cellular memory in which she had a devastating experience in another lifetime and was all alone, having been separated from her family. It was truly a traumatic experience and still recorded in the cells in her body. It was comforting to have an explanation of her distress, even if David had dismissed it as 'nothing'. As Drunvelo kept talking, her eyes opened wider and wider and she could feel her mind expanding.

Boy, if David thought the ashram was out of the box, then he will think this stuff is out of this world—literally! Dutifully she took notes and discussed the material with others who had come from all over the world to hear him.

"Hi Tori," someone called from across the room. She looked around to see who it might be and soon realized the vaguely familiar face was that of an astrologer and *vivation breathwork* specialist she had met at the ashram. She asked Peggy for a session, and within the hour Tori was settled onto a bed in the hotel as Peggy explained this work. While akin to a prenatal exercise, it was an intense circular breathing practice that would take thirty minutes before she experienced or saw anything. Tori closed her eyes, not knowing what to expect, and began the rhythmic breathing as instructed. She was astounded as she began to see whirling and swirling circles like the rings of Saturn. They were dark gray, with bubbles and gravel, and extended the width of the room. Looking out at the edge of the rings she saw a tiny image. What was so astounding to her was that it looked like a Cro-Magnon man wearing the skin of an animal—more like a spotted one-shoulder garment just like in the natural history museums. The image continued for a few more minutes until it faded away, and the session ended. Excited, she asked Peggy, "Could you see that?" She answered *yes*, and Tori laughed as she paid and gave Peggy a hug. "Thank you for that amazing experience. I will never forget it!"

On the way home Tori wondered, "Now, how much of this do I tell David? Maybe I'd better be quiet until I can process this. I'm not quite sure what I think of all this, myself."

The subject was never to come up. When she got home, news of her mother's cancer thrust her into the role of caregiver as she lovingly saw her mother through her last days.

Interlude, Luca Takes his Vows

Luca was ready. For years now he had studied, meditated, gone on pilgrimages, met with his guru, and instructed some of the new devotees. He knew all of the rituals, the prayers, the songs. It had been his life for so long that it was hard to remember the person he had been, that brash and confident young man who had everything going for him, or so it seemed. The war took away all of that and left instead an empty vessel into which the light of the spirit had poured. No longer was there yearning for the beautiful woman he could never have, no longer was the fire of ambition in his eyes. Instead he yearned only for God, and to bring whatever enlightenment he could to a world hungry for love and peace. Attaining higher consciousness was the answer, not only for himself but for those who were open to the path. The world was in turmoil, as it always seemed to be; but the heart need not be, he had discovered. Peace could be found there under the most trying circumstances, and he was willing to spend his life in helping others find that.

Interlude, The Years Between

Life had become a kaleidoscope for me, a phantasmagoric experience as I look back on it. Workshop followed workshop, class followed class, esoteric happenings followed esoteric happenings. The image of the little Cro-Magnon man was something I still haven't figured out. I guess it doesn't matter. Maybe it was time travel, or an assurance that we are all one, in spite of how and where we are. Who knows? What I do know is that it all became a matter of focus and balance.

David was busy as usual with his work, his golf buddies, our travel with friends or for business, or spending time with the next generation of family. The man may have changed his focus a bit, but he never slowed down. There were times when I was exhausted, keeping up with my activities as well as living with this human dynamo. I don't think I ever really recovered physically from that breakdown all those years ago, and I'm not sure anyone could keep up with him, anyway.

Once when we were in Seattle, we were looking through a window in a lock. It had been set up for tourists to observe the ritual of salmon returning to their birthplace. I watched one of the fish resting a minute before he swam on. He was very old and had been swimming against the current for a very long time. His gills were ripped and ragged, and I really connected with that salmon in his struggle to go home. Lifting the layers of karma was like walking on a razor's edge, and it was painful. Our ultimate destination is to be part of the divine consciousness, but it sometimes can take some doing to get there. Like swimming upstream against the current, it is the spiritual path home to the heart of the being that is often far from easy.

I can't complain, though. My life was very full and interesting; and the urge to create, to design never left me. From time-to-time Anna Mae and I had gone beyond our ideas for yoga clothing and created one-of-a-kind designs for women in town who wanted something beautiful and unique for a special occasion. Once we made the outfits for a local charity benefit, and we were happy to help with their cause; but we decided never again—too much work and too costly. Anna Mae was in demand as a seamstress, though, and that kept her as busy as she needed or wanted to be.

Esther and Mindy and I floated in and out of each other's lives, sharing confidences and news, and sometimes attending a workshop together. One we all particularly liked was a workshop where we studied the rainbow of colors and functions of the chakras, and how color can heal. For instance, each of the seven chakras has its own color: the first is red, the second is orange, the third is yellow, the four is green, the fifth is blue, the sixth is violet, and the last is indigo. Above that is a golden light that connects us to the universe. Working with a chakra that is out of balance is a way to heal our physical or emotional bodies.

In addition, we learned which color to wear each day to honor a particular spiritual being. Esther laughed, "How many colors of jeans or khakis are there?" as she mocked her usual daily attire. But I was willing to give it a try and started by wearing a ribbon on my bra, then gradually adding outfits of different colors to wear each day of the week. Now it's just automatic, and I can tell what day it is by looking at what I have on. If it's green, it's Thursday. I also started using different colored candles on the altar in order to honor the higher octave masters on the metaphysical plane: Archangel Michael, Saint Germaine, Uriel, Arcturus, Gabriel, Raphael, and Ezekiel.

I needn't have worried about David's reaction to all of this, however. One day he walked into the room as I was smiling and waving the incense around, lighting the candles, ringing the bells, and singing the chants. He stopped for a minute, bemused, then commented, "What you are doing is harmless," as he went on his way.

It was not easy getting to that place of acceptance, either for him or for me, but it does say something about the power of love. What I learned through those years of devotion and study and self-reflection was that the bottom line is love—forgiveness, love, and respect for your own self, as well as for others. And perhaps grace. There really was no other way.

Chapter 37

THE phone rang just as they were sitting down to dinner, a birthday celebration for a friend. David said, "I'll get it," and mouthed to Tori, "it's your father." She told him to tell Jacob to call back a little later, and they sat down to their meal. After the guests had departed, David and Tori were cleaning up the kitchen when the phone rang again. Drying her hands, she picked up and it was her brother. "Daddy's in the hospital for a heart attack. He and Mae were on their way to the old folks home when it happened." Jacob and Mae went every Wednesday to play *bingo with the old folks*, as he called it. He was eighty at the time.

Her relationship with her father had always been somewhat distant. It had been difficult for her to forgive him for not protecting her from her mother. He never berated her or treated her unkindly, but she felt betrayed by his allegiance to her mother. Mae changed all that. After her mother's death, Jacob had married a wonderful, beautiful woman who taught him how to show his love for his daughter, encouraging kisses and big hugs.

Since Mae was there with her father, and Tori felt it was best to let him rest, she went upstairs to bed soon after the dishes were finished. She got into bed after her usual undressing and washing ritual and put her head on the pillow, when the strangest thing happened. Like a waking dream, a macaw spoke in her head. The bird said, "You're not tired, you're not tired." It took a few minutes for this to register. When it did, she got out of bed, put on socks and a robe—why, she didn't know—and padded down the hall to the small den which was often used for a place to rest. She lay down on the sofa and never considered going to the hospital; she was sure she would see her father the next day. Turning on the light, she picked up the book she was reading at the time: *Darshan with Baba, Book III*. Each word went straight to her heart, soothing and calming her into a peacefully drowsy state. Reaching to turn off the light, she noticed two silhouettes of Baba and the enlightened guru, Nityananda, above the door to the closet in front of her! Her thoughts went immediately to her father and his life and what he gave to family and community, his goodness and kindness. Tori spoke out into the dark to him, and in a moment of transformation she saw herself standing by her father's hospital bed. "Daddy, if you hear me, blink your eyes." Her father lifted his head toward her and smiled. He seemed miles away and drifting farther. Kissing his forehead, she told him if he could not wait for her to come to the hospital tomorrow, she would understand. She wiped tears from her eyes and his face as a phone call broke their connection. It was her brother with news of Jacob's passing. She burst into tears of gratitude, feeling so blessed by the appearances of Baba and Nityananda. Her father had passed over the River of Karma, and the gurus had come to assist his crossing. That is what Sod Gurus can do! He was gone, but Tori knew there was no death. He had just stepped over the barrier, and now he was living in the light of love, truly happy and at peace.

Interlude, Goodbye to Dorothy and Max

Every life has its share of losses; and even though we sometimes flippantly say 'we all die', some losses are harder than others. This is the way it was when my dear in-laws passed. Max was the first to go when a lingering illness turned into pneumonia; and though he fought valiantly, he was not strong enough to ward it off. And maybe he was ready, anyway. His health had not been good for some time.

After the funeral, some of us went out to Old Forge, the scene of so many happy times. In earlier years there were parties with family and friends as we ate wonderful food Dorothy made, and then afterwards we all went out and played on the lake.

In winter when snow lay deep around the cottage, we shared lovely evenings as the exertion of the day's skiing morphed into welcome rest before the warmth of the fire and rosy faces filled with love.

As we opened the door this time, a fly buzzed noisily into the room, and I stopped short. I could hear Max's usual commentary on the fly situation at the lake when the children ran in and out, leaving the door open. When someone complained about the number of the annoying pests (the flies, not the children), Max would announce to the crowd, "There's not a single fly in here—they're all married!" Amidst the general laughter that echoed from that time, I knew he was with us, and it was comforting.

But then dear Dorothy passed, too, a stroke carrying her away in such haste, it took my breath and broke my heart. David and I stood on either side of her, holding her hands as she passed. Orphaned at six, she still carried that fear of abandonment, and we wanted to comfort her as best we could in her final hour.

How could I live without her wisdom, her love, her companionship? My own mother could never do what Dorothy had done for me—teach me how to be a friend, a mother, a woman. She was my lighthouse as I sailed from port to port but always came home to her steady beam. I felt as bereft as a child and wept copiously.

Then one day while I was looking for some papers in a seldom-used drawer, I came upon some old letters I had saved. Among them was one from Dorothy, written to me on Mother's Day a long time ago. As I smoothed the wrinkled paper, I had to smile. Remembering her love did not make me sad. Instead, I realized how fortunate I was to have had her in my life and to know that her spirit would always be with me.

Her life was a study in love, of course, but having that letter from her meant the world to me. She never failed to express her love and appreciation to everyone. This will show you what I mean:

> Dear Tori,
> Mere words fail to express my love for you.
> You have brought me great joy and happiness.
> If the moon and the stars had anything to do in bringing you to us, I thank them.
> Love and kisses,
> Mother

Someone once asked the Dalai Lama what was his religion, and he said 'kindness.' That could be said of Dorothy, too. Her stated religion was Orthodox, but her heart and soul simply oozed kindness to everyone she met. No one would remember the rituals she observed so faithfully, but they would remember the small and large acts of devotion to her friends and family she performed every day. I try to remember that if I miss a prayer, or neglect some other rite that I usually follow. Love, kindness, and respect for others—that is the greatest religion.

Chapter 38

THE unthinkable had happened. The twin towers of the World Trade Center had been attacked. Anyone who was breathing would never forget where they were that September 11th morning. When the towers came down in a choking cloud of smoke, dust, and debris, it seemed as if the whole city had fallen in. After a memorial was proposed some months later, David was called to be on a regional planning committee to begin generating ideas. Apparently his work in their town—a new country club, the Jewish Community Center, the first New York charter in 50 years for a new bank, all scrupulously devoted to fair and equal opportunities—had not gone unnoticed. David had always promoted non-judgmental and inclusive practices in whatever he did. It had earned him a sterling reputation, and he was well-known and much-admired.

After the regional committee had consolidated their ideas, David was called to a larger committee. This meeting in New York City was held in an older building that often housed groups dedicated to promoting peaceful activities. David was surprised to see people from foreign countries in addition to those from other parts of the United States. These included representatives wearing business suits, casual clothes, colorful ethnic attire, long skirts, women with veils, and two robed gentlemen who looked Middle Eastern. Looking around the table, David thought *this is the way it should be.* They all were aware that the process of bringing the memorial to fruition would be a long one, and they were eager to begin the project as soon as possible.

Tori asked him about the trip when he got home, and he filled her in on all the details. "And Tori, there was someone there who looked a bit like that young fellow who used to be your photographer when you had your business in New York. Wasn't his name Luca?"

Her heart gave a little jump. How long had it been since she had thought of him? The memory was like pulling pictures out of a scrapbook to look at some long-ago event, the pages yellowing now but coming into focus in the light. "Oh, really?" she asked in feigned casualness. "What did he look like?"

When David described a man with a beard and wearing robes like a religious person of some kind, maybe a monk, she immediately said, "Oh, that wouldn't be Luca; he wouldn't be wearing any kind of robe like that."

But David was not convinced. "hmmm… something about his voice……"

The diverse group of committee members, after setting their goals and general outline, returned home to do the preliminary work. They spoke with their local community leaders, drafted proposals, and communicated primarily via e-mail. David was excited about his involvement in something so close to his heart, as his humanitarian work had always vied with his business for his attention and sense of accomplishment. Tori told him how proud she was of him, and he accepted her praise with equanimity. "I was just doing what anybody would do," but she corrected him. "No, David, not just anybody," she told him emphatically. "This is your heart's work. I do believe we all have a purpose in coming to this planet, and I know this is yours. I am so happy you have this opportunity, sweetheart."

A year later when a call went out to the memorial committee to reconvene, David couldn't go. He had just been diagnosed with cancer. It was a blow, not just because of the disease, but because he knew he wouldn't be able to complete what he had just started. Always a man of action who finished, with precision, anything he ever undertook, this news almost brought him to his knees. But he knew he had to be strong for his family, and the arduous trek began.

Interlude, Renewing Wedding Vows

That kind of news always knocks anyone for a loop, no matter how much we have learned and taken to heart the feelings about death and dying, about knowing we are just renting this body for a while. We really are spiritual beings having a human experience, but the human experience can have its share of pain and loss. This was hard. David and I had made such strides over the years in our often-difficult relationship that only love could hold together.

Now, facing the loss of this life partner, it seemed so unfair: we had done so much work, and now he was dying. But of course, it wasn't fair or unfair; it was just the next step in our being together. And then I had an idea.

When we married in New York, it was in a short, simple, and somewhat impersonal ceremony. It was legal, of course, but the hastily put together affair lacked something that I had always missed as the years went by. So I suggested to David that we have another ceremony, this time to renew our wedding vows in front of our closest friends and with a rabbi who knew and loved us. He agreed.

Through my various studies over the years I had come to appreciate ceremony even more, understanding that it stood as a physical manifestation of deeper meanings which lay underneath. We both talked with the rabbi, and I issued invitations to those I knew who would want to be with us. David had a new suit, which looked wonderful on him, and a new shirt and tie. I designed an ivory satin dress, which Anna Mae made for me, with satin buttons and a bit of lace trim at the bodice. It was beautiful. We were beautiful.

I almost felt like a bride, looking at this handsome man I had shared so many years with, and wondering why he had chosen me. Then I remembered what an astrologer had told me at the beginning of our marriage: it was in the stars for us to meet and marry, no matter how difficult it might seem at times. Yes, we were meant to be together. David, for his part, smiled almost shyly at me as we began. I knew I had no regrets.

The day was perfect in every way, and it will always be one of my most cherished memories. Dear Esther was there, alone now as Arthur had passed the year before; Mindy and her children; Anna Mae, beaming like a mother of the bride; David's friends from the synagogue, including his best golfing buddies; my loyal friends from the Jewish Women's Circle; our travel companions. Our children could not attend, and of course our parents were gone, but we knew that all of them were there in spirit. We could feel their presence and honored them in the ceremony. Then we had a feast with wine and dancing and felt like newlyweds again.

Let me share now those wedding vows with you.

'David, as I stand before a different person who loved you the first time we married (now short hair, no glasses), I am the same person who loved you the first time we married. And I love you more because I really know you. I am the person you supported with more than money and pearls and diamonds, with a career and children. We are the result of the trust you gave to me when I stepped out of the box and went to the ashram to seek the knowledge of truth. You have shared this quest and ultimately received the benefits of knowing that love really is the truth and the bottom line.

I have asked the people who love us the most to witness this renewal because I know they know how special we are to each other, and how special we are to them.

This life is a blink; it's really a long dream—and sometimes a bit more. Nevertheless, it is a divine play, and we are the stars of our own drama. We have outstanding daughters who support us, and grandchildren who love us.

We invite friends to dinner to celebrate our good fortune. In return, we give love to the universe, which rejoices with us and supports our lives with blessing and abundance.

We are truly blessed, even though our children and parents are not here. They surround us on the walls with good wishes for our future years in good health, until we join them in joy.

I want to thank you again for allowing me this moment to have a wedding and a ceremony with meaning, with a rabbi who loves us and knows us and talks to us with knowledge and love. When we had our simple ceremony all those years ago, I didn't know how I would pine for a true ceremony—not the large wedding, but a meaningful and prayerful consecration.

I love you, David. There are no words that have been invented. You are beyond good.'

The 10 Commandments for Marriage:

In the beginning one became two.
Then two became one.

1. One shall love thy partner as thyself.
2. One shall show love and respect at all times
3. One shall seek to know the uniqueness of the partner or the mate.
4. One shall have patience and calmness when discussing ideas.
5. One shall be open and share feelings with trust.
6. One shall not make comparisons to another.
7. One shall be present for the other while sharing ideas and concepts.
8. One shall have honor and respect for all family members.
9. One shall understand that all situations are a reflection of one's own mind and heart.
10. One shall show appreciation for all gifts given with love, including weekly remunerations.

Chapter 39

DAVID knew he would soon die. After surgeries, alternative healing remedies, doctors' offices, pain, journeys to hospitals in New York and Boston, and untold numbers of medications, he knew the cancer had won. He was tired of the fight, and he was ready to go. Tori's financial security was in place—he had seen to that. He even took her to Boston to meet with his investment company to make sure she understood everything. Attentive as always to details, he wanted to ensure a smooth transition.

As for what might come after his death, he and Tori had talked about that, too. David was inclined to feel that doing good deeds and living a good life on earth were more important that what might come after. Tori believed in a thin veil between this world and the next. She felt that life *here* was a waking dream, and that connection with spirit transcended all worlds. For her there was no death.

But no matter what he or she believed, there was little to ameliorate the immediate pain of separation. They admitted that their relationship had had its ups and downs, but in the end they had come to a total love and acceptance of each other. Often they had had parallel lives, David with his clients and his golf friends, and Tori engaged in her spiritual pursuits. Together, they lived in town during the week and hung out in Old Forge most weekends. That was their way of life, and they had both adapted to it. It had been just the two of them for a long time now.

Since David had been diagnosed with cancer, Tori had been doing everything she could to keep him living as long as possible. He knew she would, and he was touched by her efforts. Tori had asked her healer friend, Neila, for help, and she prescribed for David a regimen of natural remedies. But he wouldn't take them. Tori tried to get him to forego some of the fatty and sweet foods he loved, but to no avail. It was too late for him to change his diet, he told her, but he did agree to try another surgery.

The girls came to New York, leaving husbands and children at home. The four of them ate Chinese food (David's favorite that Tori had introduced him to on their first date). Their bond as a family was never stronger, as they talked and played games and hid their worried looks behind bright smiles. In spite of the risks of surgery, no one had anticipated the outcome. The operation was a success, but the patient had not survived. Resuscitation could not bring him back. Tori gave him a last kiss as she bent over his lifeless body. The biggest surprise, though, was that when she went to view him in his casket, he looked just as he did when they first met! It was truly a miracle, to have her last glimpse of him looking like a young man.

Tori could not believe that he was gone—this man, so vital and alive, a *whirlwind* of a human being—dead. Time passed in a dream of calling friends and relatives, arranging the funeral. Her daughters, though devastated, stood strong beside her, but she still felt very alone. There was comfort from family and friends—phone calls and invitations and gifts of food and flowers—but at night the big house echoed only with memories. She missed the trivial things: the sound of his shoes on the floor, the clearing of his throat after he laughed. Their house seemed cold and empty as she sat wondering *just where is home?* The loss of parents, cousins, some friends, and now her husband had diminished her social life. The few left were scattered here and there, and she didn't need her big house for accommodating them or for the big parties she used to throw.

An idea slowly began to take form as she looked around her living room. Mentally she began to take stock of what she wanted and needed, and what could go. She looked at her belongings as though they were only memories and strangers, and suddenly a move felt right. She would go to David's family house, the second home they had always called their healing place. They had just begun a remodel of the Old Forge cottage. Both sets of parents were gone, but David and Tori's still-young families needed more room when they came for visits. The little red boat that David always used to take the grandchildren for rides up and down the channel sat rocking gently at the dock, and the loons cried out at dusk as if to say *come home.*

Old Forge was her haven, her place of peace, always. Tori began to envision how she would update the cottage which was filled with so many rich, warm pockets of joy and comfort. Her old designing skills awakened as she began to think of color and fabrics, building materials and hardware, the flow of energy and the capture of light. It would take most of a year; but when it was done, it would be *perfect.*

On a tender May morning she moved in, ready to unpack. The lake was sparkling, and a few boats were already on the water. A number of the summer people had drifted back. Soon they would be there in full force, and the little town would come alive again.

I will, too. Marriage designed my whole life; but now it's time to create my own pattern, this time out of whole cloth.

Interlude, Adjusting

There was a lot of rain that spring and summer *after my move. Early morning fog drifted across the lake until nearly 11 o'clock, delaying the departure of the boats that charted their paths up and down the water. I sat with my coffee in the little sun room, or sunless room I began to call it, and waited for…what?*

My children had long flown the nest, and David was in that place of peace and light he told me about in that first visitation. He came to visit often in my dreams, and sometimes I could feel his presence in the corner of the living room. But I was a widow now, and it wasn't an easy adjustment. I had always lived with someone: my parents, roommates, David, our own little family. Now it was just I, Tori. Thank heavens for the telephone. I could at least keep in touch with everyone far and near, and I did.

I can't tell you I didn't think about sex. David and I had not had the most exciting sex life, but we didn't know anything then about the spiritual side of that intimacy. We did have affection, and I missed that. I could understand even better now why the children always wanted their stuffed animals in bed with them. It was something warm and cuddly and kept them from being so lonely. I thought about getting one, and then thought about what the kids would say. Or maybe not, who knows?

Clearly I had to get on with my life, so of course I thought of something I could design. The grounds around the cottage had not really been developed. David and I never seemed to have enough time; either we were there only on weekends, or the kids were there in the summer, and who had time for something like that then? So I called around, found a landscaper, and we set to work. In no time I could see the transformation as he planted roses and bushes and filled the pots on the deck with bright summer blooms. It cheered me up no end, and of course all the plants loved the rain, so there wasn't much maintenance to do.

Then one day there was a letter in the mailbox, advertising a workshop by Drunvalo Melchizedek. I remembered the time I went to hear him in Texas, and thought, I could use a trip to Arizona. And maybe he has some new things to talk about; it sure looks like it from this brochure. My next brainstorm was to call Esther. Jack ran the farm now with help from one of Mindy's sons, and Esther had stepped back from the day-to-day maintenance. Maybe she would like a diversion? A few phone calls later, and plans were laid. I looked around the cottage and realized I didn't really have anything to wear to Arizona. I took care of that with some fabric I had been saving, sat down at my machine, and soon had something suitable and, of course, unique. It was time to get moving again.

Chapter 40

ANOTHER workshop, another approach; I can only trust that this one will continue to expand my knowledge and understanding. Meeting Baba that first time changed my life, and it has continued to change. It's always interesting, these trips, and I always get to meet interesting people, too. I'm sure this will be the same.

The desert air in Sedona was clear and dry, and the sun surrounded everything with a light that illuminated even the darkest corner. Tori and Esther were enchanted already, and the workshop hadn't even begun. People from all over the world were filtering in; and they heard greetings in such a variety of accents and languages, their heads were constantly turning.

There had been much talk around the world for some years now about what was going to happen in the year 2012. Some feared that it would be the end of the world due to cataclysmic events. Others took a more optimistic view that what was really happening was a dramatic change in consciousness. Many of the people attending were seeking esoteric knowledge, answers to their questions about this time in history.

Tori shared a similar interest with these people and especially with the remarkable man that was leading the workshop, Drunvalo Melchizedek. At the last workshop Tori attended, he told them about his travels to over 70 tribes, teachers, and gurus around the world in order to clarify his understanding of these events. He also explained to the group that he had actually come in as 'walk-in', inhabiting a body volunteered by an individual for that purpose. He spoke of coming down from the 13th dimension into the 3rd, and polarity consciousness was unknown to him. *Was he real? Was he telling the truth? Did he have amazing insights? Or was he just a little crazy? They could decide soon enough.*

Drunvalo was aware of all of these concerns, and had been for some time; but he was an innocent, and his teaching reflected that. There was something almost child-like in his demeanor, joyous, very present in the moment. It was refreshing and engaging as he stated that everyone was part of God, and that the illusion of separation was just that—an illusion.

He turned more serious, though, as he talked about the true purpose of this teaching—ascension. It seems that most of humanity is now living in the third dimension. But now that human consciousness is accelerating into a new height of understanding, it is possible to ascend in spirit into the fifth dimension. When that occurs, memory will not be lost as it was 13,000 years ago but remain intact, so that knowledge and spiritual growth will not have to be remembered or relearned.

Merkaba

Tori had read his books before she came to the workshop; so she was familiar with the language of light bodies, the Mer-Ka-Ba, star tetrahedrons, cellular memory and the mystery schools. The Mer-Ka-Ba meditation was fascinating to her, especially the information that the energy of light bodies stretches out fifty or more feet. This particular meditation was said to be helpful in attaining the ascension Drunvelo talked about. The books were very difficult for Tori to completely absorb; she knew the information in her DNA, but retrieving it was a different story.

But sitting there in the group listening to him was like being bathed in luxurious warmth and love, especially when he began to talk about living in the heart. That is when it all clicked for her, and she had a certain sense of knowing that this was truth. This made sense in a very real way; her friendship with Esther attested to that. She turned to Esther, and they smiled at each other in a deep and very knowing way; Esther gave her hand a squeeze that assured her that all was well.

Later their class walked among the beautiful rocks to a spot higher up the mountain where they enjoyed a panoramic view of the valley. It was awe-inspiring to view the valley floor give way to the rich red of the rocks that sprang up in varying formations. The group had hiked there to do a special meditation, and Tori felt that just being in all that natural beauty was a meditation in itself. Just before the sun set and the first stars pricked the still-luminous sky, she gave thanks—to the universe, to the fortunes that brought her here, for the opportunity to open her heart still wider, and to travel farther down the road on this most amazing journey to awakened consciousness. *And thank you, too, David, she said as if in prayer. You really made this possible with your hard work and generosity. Thank you.*

Chapter 41

WHILE attending the workshop in the desert, Tori met Liz. There was an instant connection between them. In fact, they both felt as if they knew each other deeply—perhaps even in another lifetime. In their conversation one evening after class, Liz asked Tori if she had heard of Patricia Cota-Robles. When Tori shook her head, she told her about a convocation she had attended and how impressed she was. This woman talked about raising consciousness to the next level, the Company of Heaven who was assisting her and all mankind, preparation for ascension, and many other things. She said her nearly week-long workshops included lots of music, guest speakers on important topics, relevant and unusual videos, and incredibly powerful meditations. In fact, Liz said, the first one she attended was so powerful that she actually levitated off her chair for a few seconds. "You really must meet her, Tori. It will truly change your life." Liz promised to send Tori a tape of a very powerful meditation called *The Violet Flame*. "Just listen to it all the way through, and then call me. I guarantee you it will knock your socks off."

When Tori got home, she had forgotten about the CD her new friend had promised to send. So it was a pleasant surprise to receive it in the mail with a lovely card from her new *old* friend. That evening as she got ready for bed, she put the CD in the player and lay back on her bed to listen. The night was dark with scudding clouds. Now and then the light of the quarter moon broke through and lit the room for just an instant before it disappeared again. Tori hardly noticed, as her breathing had changed, and she fell into a very deep meditation. When the meditation ended Tori basked in the calm and serenity filling her complete being. That night she experienced a deep and dreamless sleep that seemed eternal, and she woke the next day feeling like a new woman.

Chapter 42

Tori was sitting on the deck with her knitting, a pastime she had begun when her first grandchild was born, and she had made an afghan for each successive baby. After that she hadn't had time for it, but recently she had taken up the craft again. It was a good activity when she was watching TV, or waiting for someone to arrive; or just enjoying the rays of the sun that fell long and golden between the now-tall pine trees.

When the phone rang, she went to answer it. An unfamiliar voice asked, "Are you Mrs. David Litchfield?" The voice on the other end, filled with compassion and respect, requested her presence in New York City to accept a posthumous award for her husband's work on the 9/11 memorial committee. Tori hung up the phone after accepting, filled with trepidation. Would there be lots of people there? Would she know anyone? How would it feel to accept this for David? Could she contain her emotions? And, of course, what would she wear? Not black, she ruled out instantly. *I'm not going as a widow.*

She chose instead a pretty purple and teal outfit with a matching scarf she had bought last summer on a whim. For her jewelry she wore a diamond bracelet of Dorothy's that Max had given her for their anniversary. Her earrings were pearls set in gold that had been one of David's last gifts. *I can do this*, she told herself, as the train wound its way down through the mountains and valleys and into the city.

David had told her that there were representatives from many faiths and countries on the committee, all coming together to establish an inclusive interfaith memorial. Peace and forgiveness—the world needed that. She was happy and honored to take part, filled with pride for David and all that he had accomplished in his life. How surprising it was to her sometimes to consider the man that the public knew, in comparison to the man who was her husband. She was happy that over the years there had been reconciliation, love, and acceptance of each other and their individual gifts and talents.

When Tori arrived at the meeting, she scanned the room and marveled at the variety of dress from dignitaries from different countries. She was in heaven taking in the garments embroidered in gold and the peacock blue saris and redesigning them in her head for American fashion. The most regal-looking man was the one standing with his back to her in his robes and turban. She wondered what Arabic country he came from. That must be the man David mentioned, Tori decided, the one he said looked like Luca. He did have a similar build, and for a few moments she allowed herself the indulgence of dreaming that it was her Lawrence of Arabia. The gentleman turned toward her and then back to excuse himself from the conversation in which he was involved. She felt caught in a dream as he gracefully walked towards her, his robes brushing the marble floors. In front of her he stopped and bowed, taking both her hands in his as he lifted his eyes to hers.

"Hello, Tori."

Oh my! David had been right. It was Luca! How could this be possible? "Luca" was all she could say as she looked deeply into his eyes filled with wisdom gained from the experiences of a long and hard life. The beard was new, and there were lines that had not been there all those years ago; but the voice and his bright white smile she would know anywhere. There was great kindness in his face, and the compassion in his eyes reminded her of Baba. They stepped apart then as the meeting was called to order, and the business of the award ceremony was conducted. Tori was barely able to stay grounded, so overcome was she with emotions.

She did manage to direct her attention to the front of the room. When they called her name to come up to accept David's award, she saw how much love he received in his lifetime; how much of his time and energy he had spent in higher service. It made her so proud. He had truly been the epitome of one who did good works, and his path was just as valid as hers.

Stepping down from the podium, Luca guided her to a table where they spent the evening sharing their stories and arranging a longer visit. Tori suggested he come down to Old Forge for a couple of days until he had to leave the country again. "I took the train down, but when we're there I'll give you a ride in that little red roadster David had. I don't know if you remember, but I had it restored and tool around town in it." He laughed and took her up on the offer.

Once again Old Forge performed its primary functions as haven and healer as their stories unraveled the mystery of their time apart. While describing their spiritual journeys, they were both astonished at the connection they both had with Muktananda. Their paths had diverged somewhat, as Luca had become a swami, and Tori had sought out a variety of teachers. "But Tori, we see that they all led to the same end," Luca said gently as they sipped their tea. He looked around at the comfortable living room with its pleasing colors, and then out over the water. "This beautiful and peaceful place you have here is as much of a retreat as my ashram in India. They both serve the same purpose: opening peoples' hearts, healing them, teaching divine love, bringing into oneness all those who enter. It happens in myriad ways."

Tori was pleased that he caught the spirit of her favorite place and suggested that they walk down to the water. "The loons like to call to each other at this time of day," she told him, as the cries of the strikingly-marked birds echoed eerily against the shoreline.

"How's Gabriella?"

"I hear she is not well. I have to be in Malta to take care of some business on my way home, and I plan to see her while I'm there."

"I still remember vividly our trip to the Sleeping Lady. That experience was the beginning of a big change in my life. I've never known how to repay her for that. Please tell her hello for me and I'd love to see her again. I've always wanted to go back to Malta, but for years it wasn't possible; and I wasn't ready. Now I could, though!"

They went inside to make dinner, and he surprised her with some curry to try with the rice and vegetables she had made. They lingered over more tea and the special coconut ice cream Tori served and talked late into the night. She recited a story of doing *seva* at the ashram where Baba, with 12 people around the table, was making a special meal that included potatoes. First they had to mash them gently with their hands, and then they were to put them into serving-sized cups after Baba had seasoned them with a blend of herbs. She wasn't paying attention; and soon the little cups were not in a straight line, as directed, but all over the place. It reminded Tori of an *I Love Lucy* episode involving an assembly line. Flustered, Tori said she didn't know what to do until she remembered to say the mantra *Om Namah Shivya* that was chanted all the time there. It was the mantra that created the energy frequency of the ashram, like tuning into a radio station. The power of it was all-encompassing, and it drew her into her heart. Given that focus, the cups realigned themselves. "True story!" she laughed.

Luca told some of his stories, too, including one about a wise man who greeted each event in his life, no matter how hard or beautiful or complicated, with a simple *so be it*. "We have both had our challenges, Tori, but surrendering to God and to whatever the universe sends us is the key." He told her how much that bit of wisdom had meant to him as he struggled to find his guru, and then to prepare for and walk the spiritual path he had chosen. He would not talk about Vietnam, though, and she didn't ask.

The next morning, after morning prayers, they shared breakfast before he prepared to leave. Tori had arranged for someone to pick him up and drive him to the train, so they would say their goodbyes now.

"Be sure to say hello to Gabriella for me."

"I'll be sure to." His eyes sought hers. "Tori, you must know I was in love with you when I was your photographer. That's one reason I never came back. But over the years I discovered a much deeper and greater love, and I feel that you have experienced that, too. "

"Yes. David was a truly good man, and he supported my search for truth and meaning in my life. We had a good and deep love. I must tell you that I loved you also, Luca, but I'm happy to say that it is divine love that I aspire toward today."

Luca took her shoulders firmly in his hands and kissed her on both cheeks.

"I always knew there was something special about you!"

Tori smiled bravely as he walked down the steps and toward the waiting car. She felt flush with emotion and filled with gratitude that she and Luca had had the opportunity to meet again. She knew she had been blessed by this remarkable man who was also her friend. Would she see him again? She didn't know, but it wasn't important. This gift of reunion was enough in itself, and she said a prayer of thanksgiving as she watched the car pull away.

Chapter 43

Luca landed in Malta in the early afternoon, and the sparkling sea and the myriad colors of the boats enchanted him. He had almost forgotten how beautiful it was here. He had not seen his godmother, Gabriella, for many years, as his visits in and out of Malta had been few, brief, and filled with business responsibilities. It was time to catch up, as she was very old now and in frail health, he had heard.

He didn't call ahead but showed up on her doorstep and rang the bell that had hung there for as long as he could remember. He heard someone inside speak in a low but clear voice, "Come in." He pushed open the door and found her lying on a chaise lounge beside a fire that had burned down to ash. She looked up at him and smiled.

"My spirit called you here. I'm glad you heard me." She nodded to Luca as he found a chair nearby and sat down beside her. "I have something to tell you, dear one, before I die—which it appears I will do very soon." She looked steadily into his eyes as she said simply, "I am your mother." He took her hand. "I know," he said softly, and his eyes shone at the words he had waited all his life to hear. "I have always known."

With that he began to cry as she stroked his head and told him the story of how she had become pregnant by his father. They were not married, and it was simply forbidden for them to marry. "Times were very different then, Luca. I hope you understand." He nodded. His father insisted that the child be raised in the family home, and he would generously support her and allow her to take the role of godmother if she would keep secret the circumstances of his birth. Knowing that this was the best course in their culture, she agreed, but as godmother she could maintain a close relationship with the child as he grew up.

Luca took up the story. His father had told him that his mother had died when he was born. When he was older, he wondered why there was no grave or headstone to visit; but his father told him he had planted the fig tree in the courtyard to honor her, instead. Later, his father married a woman from a prominent family, and two sons were born to them. His father and stepmother founded a spiritual center, which they had groomed Luca to take over. Except he went to New York instead, greatly disappointing them. After his disappearance into Vietnam and India, his brothers took leading roles and eventually took over. "After I took my orders, I went back for a brief visit before setting up my own center in India. My grandfather had died by then, of course; but when the call came for someone to represent the family at the Interfaith Memorial in New York, the family felt I should go to honor Papa's memory. He had wanted to talk to me about a project he was considering when I was in Malta long ago—do you remember that time I came as a fashion photographer?"

"Yes. I watched you and that lovely woman, Tori, and knew what lay ahead. I knew these things because I was from the ancient lineage of the priests in the old temples. I did not practice this overtly, but I did have the gift of knowing what paths people were meant to take. It's interesting that you two have sought out the spiritual life you were destined for, though in different ways; you were never meant to be together in the usual sense."

Luca agreed with a nod of his head and told her that he and Tori had just been together at an event in New York and then at her home in the country. "She asked about you and sends her love," and told her that she and Mindy and a friend of theirs wanted to return for a long-delayed visit. But as he looked into her eyes, he knew she would be gone by then, passing peacefully into the light of ultimate consciousness. He didn't cry. They both knew there was nothing to fear and only total happiness and oneness to attain.

He leaned over to kiss her on the cheek. "Goodbye, Mama, I love you."

"I love you, too, son. I am so proud of you. Give your friends my regards."

He stopped in her garden on his way out. He noticed that there was a fig tree in her yard, and wondered when that had been planted. But he shook his head and walked on with a lighter step. The last mystery had been solved.

Interlude, Post-death Visit from David

I'm not sure I told you this story. Time seems so ephemeral the older I get, and I sometimes forget if I've already told you something. David remained such a presence in my life after his death, but this episode still stays with me as though it just happened. And, I suppose, if we believe that everything is Now, then it did. But anyway, here it is.

A few weeks after the funeral, I came downstairs on a cold winter morning and made some hot coffee to take away the chill. I needed more than hot coffee, though. David's absence pervaded the house, chilling my heart and soul. I had made the decision to move to Old Forge, but I knew I would take these memories with me, and perhaps someday they would warm me again.

Taking the hot cup to the living room, I sat with my fingers wrapped around it and stared out the window, but the bare trees offered no comforting view. I uttered a deep sigh, and at that moment I felt a warm presence in the room as if my breath had stoked live embers. I turned toward the unlit fireplace as an inner voice spoke to me. There was no doubt it was David's; I would know that special timbre anywhere. I picked up a pen and notebook from my desk and waited quietly, though chills were traveling up and down my spine. I was not afraid, just excited.

'I'm with you all the time; you can feel my presence, can't you? I'm listening and learning all you have to teach me. You spoke a foreign language when we were together. I'm so sorry. I love you so. You were right—life is a waking dream, and when we truly wake up, we are in light. It's all about unconditional love, acceptance, and kindness.

'I like it that you are wearing my folding glasses. I love the way the rooms look with all the colors.

'We all watch you and how your mind moves with objects. It is beautiful to see. We have no time; it is always "now" just like you told me. I had a great partner. You deserve all I could give you, and more.'

David has come to me many times. In fact, it seemed for a while that he was with me more after his death than before! Sometimes he came to counsel about financial matters, sometimes to offer words of wisdom, but most often just to lend his presence and to make sure I was all right. He comes less frequently now, as it should be, but I have always been grateful for the lessons he taught, and for the love that we shared. It was so hard at first when he passed on, such a shock to my mortal system. Losing a loved one is enormous and all encompassing. But it helps to be open to their presence, and I always have been.

Am I crazy to say that I talk with my dead husband? I don't think so.

Chapter 44

"How many times have I stood in my closet and wondered what I was going to wear?" Tori was packing for a trip to New Zealand. She was not a light packer, and the changing climates they would be encountering made it even more of a dilemma. She had been to a World Congress led by Patricia Cota-Robles last year and was so moved that she signed up for this year's Pilgrimage. There had been something different in the air at that conference. True, there had been people coming from all over the world to other workshops she had attended. But from the very first talk and the ensuing meditation at the World Congress, her heart had opened so wide that she began to weep. And she was not the only one, she discovered, as she looked around the room. She felt as if she were surrounded by old friends, though they had never seen each other in this life before. They often fell into each other's arms, blurting out, "It's so good to see you again!"

"This is true oneness," Tori thought. "This is unity consciousness. I really get it now."

Finally packing her suitcase and managing to snap it shut, she and Esther were off to see another part of the world to experience another step in their divine journey, as they had begun to call it.

New Zealand was not like anything Tori had experienced so far. The country, the people, the sacred sites, the magical Maori, the profound meditations and Activities of Light were all nearly overwhelming in their beauty and meaningfulness.

"It was as though I was in a dream," she told Mindy on her return. Mindy had picked up Tori and Esther at the airport, and they were driving home. "Every day, at every sacred site, we seemed to be taken higher, and every few days a few meridians of the earth's crystal grid system were cleared. I can't tell you how powerful all this was! The atmosphere even spilled over into the hotels and restaurants we frequented, including the drivers of our tour buses. Everyone, it seemed, was joining in. Everyone around us was experiencing a rise in their consciousness. None of us on the tour had ever experienced anything like that. In fact, it turns out that everyone on the tour and everyone we met had contracted to be together for that time. It's hard to explain the amazing energy that continued day after day. There really are no words to fully describe it."

"But I can see it in your face, Tori. You are simply glowing. Tell me something of the things that happened, where you went, what you saw," Mindy asked.

Tori was eager to oblige. The Pilgrimage had far exceeded all of their expectations. She looked over at Esther. "Please fill in if I leave anything out.

"Well, Mindy, I don't want this to sound like a travelogue or lecture, but I will tell you what we learned just to set the stage for you. New Zealand plays a critical role in the earth's ascension process—at least, that's what Patricia teaches. Also, the country receives the first impulse of light for every new day on the planet. The islands there are the hands of Mother Earth. Since we receive and transmit energy through our hands, every acupuncture meridian associated with our chakra system is represented within the acupuncture pressure points in our hands. This light that flows in and out of us is our life force, which allows us to live, move, think, and breathe in the physical plane."

Mindy's eyes opened wide as she took that in. "I've never heard it explained that way before, and I'll certainly think about light in a different way now."

"We are called Light Workers, Mindy, because we are here to bring light to the planet. As we traveled around the country there, we met so many people, went to so many sacred sites, and were blessed by many contacts with the Maori. They even gave each of us a piece of jade carved in individual ways that they believe help with personal transformation and spiritual growth. Oh, and we went to a place called Fairy Spring; I especially thought of you there, my dear."

Mindy gave her a smile. "Thank you, Tori."

"I could go on and on, and I probably will later, but the things I want to stay focused on are the light and the miracles that are taking place every hour, every day. Lots of negativity is surfacing now so that it can be cleansed and healed. We truly are on our way to a much better world."

Esther had been quiet as Tori relayed their newest adventure, and now she spoke up. "I agree with Tori. It may seem that things are only difficult and harsh right now in many parts of the world, but this will all change; and we will all be changed with it."

When she was alone, Tori reflected on just what the difference was this time. Each workshop, each teaching, every course had led her deeper and deeper into her heart and soul. Each seemed to explain a different facet of the whole, enlightening her and healing old wounds. But she had to say, this one truly was the culmination of all of those experiences. Peaceful and fulfilled in a more profound way than she ever had before, Tori felt only gratitude for this life and excitement for what lay ahead.

Interlude, Last Thoughts

I started out thinking that this was a mystery, that I was a mystery, that life itself is a mystery. I still do, yet this story is not a whodunit. I wasn't looking for the butler who did it in the library with a rope. What I was looking for is what I think we all look for—some idea of who we are, why we are here, what we're supposed to be doing.

As for this life I've told you about, and hopefully entertained you a little on the way, I've observed that it seemed to have its own course. I really didn't plan it that way. Early on I was intrigued with life and decided to study other peoples' lives instead of my own, which I hoped would lead me to some understanding. But of course, it all led back to my own. After all, whose lives could we understand but our own?

What would possess a young woman from that Orthodox household whose grandfather was a Rabbi afraid of death to strike out on such a different path? I clearly had talent as a designer, and I have always enjoyed fashion and design and just the sheer beauty of decorating ourselves and our environments. It is something that has never left me, but I did forsake that as a career and followed instead this nebulous thing called a spiritual path. No wonder my friends wondered about me, and probably talked about me. But it became a life I loved, and I was determined to follow it to the end.

Of course, there is no end. Did I plan this life course? Well, not in the traditional sense. But I do feel it was planned for me by some higher being or consciousness, and I was compelled to go with it. I have no regrets.

It has given me a different way to think about things. For instance, once on a long flight, I noticed that planes looked a lot like whales, and I thought of those magnificent creatures that have been here for 500 million years and hold all the secrets of the earth in their DNA. Dolphins have been here for 35 million years and are second only to whales in their knowledge of the earth. And do we acknowledge that wisdom? I suppose some are beginning to, but it has been long in coming.

Change is slow and hard and subject to abrupt turns. That was true for much of my journey. But oh, the rewards—the teachers I have known, the places I have been privileged to visit, the friends I have made—are all worth it.

I remember watching a television show long after I was an adult, and they were talking about ADD and dyslexia. Bingo! Mystery solved. That was why I had so much trouble in school, in spite of being smart. So life is full of mysteries of all kinds. I hope you can solve some of your own.

Now chart your own course, or reflect on the one you have taken. Go into it with an open mind, find what works best for you, stay awake, pay attention, and be prepared to change. I remember in one of Gurumayi's talks she said, "God never says no!" Listen to your own truth and not other's. After all, your consciousness is the divine actor. Your role is written in the stars. And free will makes all the plays.

As for me, now I am going to make a cup of tea and then take my cup and this journal to the sun room and look out over the water that changes every day, but still remains a steady presence. I am so grateful, for that and for so much more.

Namaste.

Epilogue

As the little red car slowly follows a curve in the two-lane road, heavily wooded on either side, one looks at four heads visible from afar. Moving in for a close-up, you see four very different women.

One is huddled in a corner to protect her essence from the sun, bright but not all that warm in late September. All are wearing scarves that honor the colors of the day, a practice learned in one of the many workshops attended over the years.

One of them looks frail, but looks are deceiving. Caroline is Mindy's daughter with a thin build like her mother, but a fierce fire burns in her startling green eyes. She nestles on her neck pillow with a red and white broad-brimmed hat tied under her chin.

Esther, always the outdoors girl, is on the back seat beside Caroline. Widowed for some years now, she has always been an independent woman who managed her farm, her show dogs, and the rest of her life with apparent ease. Realistically, though, she now relies on her long-time farm manager, Jack, to responsibly take care of everything.

Tori is driving her convertible, not new but well-kept. It is like an extension of herself, a bonding with her deceased husband, who drove it on these same country roads when he was alive.

Mindy occupies the passenger seat. She is enjoying a break from the design company that she manages, along with riding classes she sometimes teaches to children on Esther's farm. All their thoughts now are on the latest goddess tour to be held in Malta.

Tori and Mindy had long wished to return to the island they had visited for a fashion shoot intended for *Vogue* magazine. For both it had been a unique experience. Life had not been the same for either of them since then, and they wanted to re-visit the magical place that had so altered their lives.

Esther had heard all the stories from that trip, and she wanted to see it first-hand, as well as participate in the goddess rituals Tori had told them about.

Caroline had grown up with the stories of her mother's friends as they headed off many times to various parts of the globe on their spiritual adventures. She observed that it had sometimes served each of them in a different way, but the bonding of these women was visible. Now it was her time.

Tori drove carefully, as her eyesight left something to be desired. Perhaps she should have called Harold, her driver for many years; but it was not far, and she knew the road like the back of her hand.

Another adventure, she thought. What would it bring this time? And the old excitement began to rise as she made the turn into the airport.

About the Author

Even as a young girl, Nikki was fascinated with the way colors, fabrics and shapes interacted to add visual and emotional enjoyment to the person and to the environment. From the age of 12 she began designing clothes, and rearranging furniture in ways that made her feel "alive and rich". She developed a passion for colorful clothing, and designs that were way ahead of her time. She graduated from the New York fashion academy in 1956 and successfully pursued a career in design until 1976.

But it was not until many decades later that she finally understood why form was indeed sacred, and received personal confirmation that color did affect our psyche and environment in profound ways.

Nikki's first spiritual experiences occurred in her teens and were the catalyst for her to simultaneously pursue a deeper understanding of the "Presence" that seemed to be guiding her. She always knew she had a mission beyond the world of fashion.

She learned to Meditate in the early 70's when it was still an unknown commodity to most. Spiritual development continued to hold a strong attraction for her and she realized the importance of creating an inner reality to match the beauty she saw in the outer world.

Some of her most pivotal spiritual experiences occurred during times spent under the guidance of Swami Muktananda in 1976. She subsequently spent many summers at his ashram in NY.

Her desire to seek out and understand the deepest mysteries of life led her to attend countless workshops and classes on Sacred Geometry the Merkaba, and heart opening given by Drunvalo Melchizedek, where Nikki graduated as a teacher of Sacred Geometry in 1994.

Nikki studied and taught various forms of Yoga; gained a certificate from the School of Enlightenment and Healing in 1998; and took classes through the International Academy of Mastery which included hundreds of hours of personal work with Dawn Bothie to develop and enhance her connection with inner guidance and intuition. Nikki also took seminars on astrology, Higher Self connection, and the use of the Violet Flame with a variety of teachers. She has always felt her spiritual quest was carefully guided by St. Germaine.

Her transformational experiences continue through the present day through a variety of vision quests and spiritual pilgrimages, including "Goddess" tours to Malta in 2006, 2007, 2012 and a sacred pilgrimage to New Zealand with Patricia Cote Robles in 2011.